Perception. Reputation. Powerful women are still held to a higher standard when it comes to sexual escapades, making it risky business for them to be unlucky in love.

That's where the Hirsch sisters improve the odds with their companion compatibility service. Introducing philanthropic heiresses and female executives to honorable, educated, hard-working men willing to act as sophisticated arm candy to supplement their wages becomes a shared passion project for the three sisters because their wealthy mother killed herself after being scammed by their father. So they created The LuxeLinks Club—No fortune hunters. No gold diggers.

~

When She's on Top was a 2004 IPPY Awards Finalist in the category of Erotica/Sexuality

erotic romance, whose plot has some teeth, with excellent character development, showing strong but realistic women of color, and plenty of spicy sex scenes, *When She's on Top* is one both erotic romance and romantic suspense fans should love. *~ Regan Murphy, The Review Team of Taylor Jones & Regan Murphy*

ACKNOWLEDGMENTS

Thank you to Lauri, L.P., Arwen, Jack, and the entire Team BOB. Neither Mother Nature nor plague of flu stopped them from launching *When She's on Top* into the readersphere when Murphy's Law kicked into full effect. Special thanks to editors extraordinaire Reyana and Faith.

The members of the BOB Authors' Yahoo Group educate, inspire, encourage, and challenge me to strive for more every day. Their generous camaraderie lifts my spirit with each exchange.

My parents, who've shown me how healthy loving relationships look, feel, and sound by their example, will celebrate fifty years of marriage this year. My deepest gratitude to them for laying the foundation for my life. Many thanks to my family and friends for loving me and understanding that my communications silences aren't ghosting.

Last, and most certainly not least, thank you to readers who support small and independent publishers and the authors whose voices might otherwise remain unheard.

May the love you give return to you tenfold,

C. B.

WHEN SHE'S ON TOP

The LuxeLinks Club Stories

C. X BROOKS

A Black Opal Books Publication

GENRE: EROTIC ROMANCE/ROMANTIC SUSPENSE

WHEN SHE'S ON TOP
Copyright © 2018 by C. X Brooks
Cover Design by C. X Brooks
All cover art copyright © 2018
All Rights Reserved
Print ISBN: 978-1-626948-95-2

First Publication: APRIL 2018

Published by Black Opal Books **http://www.blackopalbooks.com**

DEDICATION

*To powerful women and the men
who are strong enough to love us*

Table of Contents

This Mark Changes the Game
Page 1

This Mark Evens the Odds
Page 97

This Mark Leaps Into the Abyss
Page 169

This Mark Flips the Script
Page 229

CHAPTER 1

This Mark Changes the Game
The LuxeLinks Club Story 1

Twenty Years Ago:

Send in my next visitor, please, Nancy."

Estate planner and family trust attorney Jaime Lowenthal straightened his silk tie after using the intercom on his fancy new office phone system.

Glancing around at the freshly painted space conservatively decorated and minimally furnished with a few cast-off collectible antiques from his grandparents made him glad that he had opened his own practice instead of joining his papa's firm.

The closed door that separated his office from the

short hallway to the small reception area glided open silently.

"Here we are, Miss Hirsch and Mrs. Brown," his secretary said as she guided a young girl wearing a plaid school uniform, and an older woman in a denim shirt and overalls into his office. Nancy introduced the child as his prospective client, Miss Margeaux Carr Hirsch of the New England department stores Hirsches, and her chaperone as Mrs. Janet Brown.

Nancy waited for them to be seated before she backed out of the office and closed the door softly.

"How may I be of service to you, Miss Hirsch?"

Solemn brown eyes framed by thick lashes, much darker than the cap of toasted brown curls atop her head, stared directly into his eyes for several slow blinks. She nodded once then reached into her Wonder Woman backpack and pulled out a silver piggy bank, which she balanced in her lap.

"Daddy stole all of Mommy's money and divorced her to run off and marry a gold-digging tramp. Then Mommy killed herself because she was so sad. Now we're going to live with Daddy all the time." She paused until her lower lip stopped quivering. "Mr. Lowenthal, I need to hire you to protect my trust fund and the trust funds for my little sister, Julianna, and our baby sister, Chloe."

CHAPTER 2

Present Day:

The padded envelope was small, three inches by five according to the pre-printed details on the back just below the pull tab. She flipped the package again, and again read *Alexa Davis Spencer* in uniform block type above her residential address rendered in the same bold font on the shipping label. The return address was an unfamiliar post office box. The postmark was local.

She frowned as she tested the weight of the parcel on the palm of her hand. She hadn't ordered anything, and even so, she always shipped her deliveries to her workplace to guarantee someone was available to sign for them.

She pulled the tab. Inside, an unassuming black thumb drive with a "play me" sticky note tempted her curiosity beyond her willingness to resist. Repeated warnings from her company's mandatory quarterly seminars, about security protocols and personal safety measures, cycled through her brain while Alexa headed toward her home office at the back of her secluded residence in an exclusive suburban gated community. She located her tablet, which she used primarily as her e-reader. If the drive was infected with a virus that her high-end computer security software couldn't handle, she wouldn't lose anything that couldn't be recovered.

She curled into the window seat as the video file automatically opened. A sunny scene filled with clear blue skies and citrus trees tapped into her memories of her recent long weekend getaway at the Seaside Enclave in Florida with her secret boyfriend, artist Beckford Gallegas. When the focus swung to an ornately scrolled iron fence with the letters S and E worked into the design, Alexa's breath hitched with a sudden spike of anxiety.

The image faded to black, then dissolved into the setting of an exquisitely appointed bedroom suite. The king-sized bed held her attention, not only because it dominated the space, but because it was occupied by a woman and a man—by Alexa and Beck.

That moment of recognition split her consciousness into two levels of awareness. Horrified shock and anger and fear at the irrefutable evidence of the violation of her personal privacy, of Beck's personal privacy, rolled through her in nauseating waves. At the same time, she recognized how sensual and loving the two bodies locked together looked in the moving image. The absence of sound made their embrace appear even more explicit.

Alexa had never recorded herself having sex or permitted anyone else to record her. She had never understood the appeal of doing so. Until this moment. From the wavy fall of her disheveled hair atop her tipped back head to the rise and fall of her full lips and open mouth, down her rounded chin to the long curve of her exposed neck drawing the eye to her breasts, prominently displayed to heaving advantage encased in a pale yellow confection of lace and satin, the undulations of her body broadcast the joys of carnal abandon. Stretched along the upward curve of her deeply arched back, her softly padded ribs and her stomach contracted and expanded up and down, in and out with Beck's driving thrusts unimpeded by the crotchless panel of the lace and satin matching bottoms between her bent and spread legs.

With the soles of her feet propped against the low foot rail and one of Beck's arms coiled across her lower back to hold her perfectly angled to receive him from tip to root, Alexa watched the video and remembered every stroke. So did her body. Her nipples ached. Her clitoris ached, and the crotch of her leggings was already soaked as she watched Beck use the strength in his straight arm braced against the mattress to keep them elevated while he pivoted on the balls of both feet planted firmly on the hardwood floor.

Watching the video transported her back to that physical place and head space. The way her glutes, her thigh muscles, and calf muscles quivered from the strain of being folded and spread to cradle his pumping hips. The slick, sweaty slide of his skin over hers and the squelching squish of his erection as his balls smacked her butt. His sweat. Her sweat. Their commingled scents. On the window seat, Alexa pressed her thighs together as tightly as she could manage while dragging her sopping wet crotch against the tufted cushion for stimulating friction. Doing so aggravated her much more than it helped.

In the video, Alexa's hips rocked forward and back in opposition to Beck's rapid thrusts, slapping their sweaty flesh together. She watched herself unraveling as the strong hand clasping her hip moved to push into the back of her lacy bottoms to delve between the crease of her buttocks. One long, callous finger breached her, making her whole body jerk at the titillating discomfort. Beck sped the pace and force of his thrusts while screwing his finger deeper into her bottom until she felt on the verge of splitting apart from the overwhelming pressure of fullness.

As she observed her past pleasures, Alexa stretched one leg along the window seat and the other with her foot on the floor, spreading her legs and leaning back against the window. One hand held her tablet. The other reached under her running t-shirt, into the waistband of her leggings and used two fingers to penetrate the gushing wetness of her vagina while her thumb stroked her clitoris.

In the silent video, it was clear from their facial expressions and body gyrations that she and Beck were uninhibitedly vocalizing the escalation of their imminent orgasms.

Alexa remembered Beck's hot breath in her ear. His grunts and groans and incoherent exclamations as he'd forged deeper and harder into the heart of her desire had loosened her own grunts and cries when he worked another big finger into her tight anal chute and launched her into screaming, shuddering orgasm.

In that moment and in this, she felt her internal muscles clamp down hard on the thickness between her legs, squeezing tighter and tighter while her clitoris pulsed with each glancing stroke. The gateway to her womb contracted and released, milking Beck's hard erection in the past and her two fingers in the present. Then and now, she creamed hard as she writhed and panted in sexual ecstasy.

❧❦❧

Alexa paused the video playback to change her clothes, to spot clean her body and the seat cushion with a little mild soap and water, then she got comfortable sitting in lotus pose on the floor of her home office.

Masturbating had taken the edge off her excitement, allowing her to watch the remaining fifteen minutes of imagery with a measure of clinical detachment. There was still no audio, and the camera angle appeared fixed to cover the length of the bed from headboard to a little beyond the foot rail, from only a few feet above the mattress to the floor.

"Focus on the details," she whispered under her breath when watching Beck as he collapsed atop her, but kept thrusting while executing a slight pushup and a tilt of his head to put his mouth at the perfect angle to suckle one of her breasts nearly derailed her attention away from the practical aspects. Remembering the hot, damp suction of his mouth pressing soft lace and satin against her stiff nipple threatened to lure her into more self-pleasuring, but Alexa forced herself to maintain a two-handed grip on the tablet, even though watching him turn his head to suckle her other breast flashed the sensation of beard stubble dragging across the soft mounds of her heaving breasts.

"Focus, Alexa," she whispered again.

The video ended after running for a total of thirty minutes before fading to black. While the runtime counter kept ticking off seconds, Alexa sorted her thoughts. Her observations about the fixed camera angle and limited scope in addition to the short duration of this recording of what she knew had been their first intimate encounter as soon as they checked into their isolated bungalow suggested a motion-sensor trigger to start recording.

"Alexa Davis Spencer, CEO of Universal Tapestry Group, a Fortune One Hundred company," a computer-generated voice spoke calmly from her tablet. The screen remained black except for the runtime counter.

Knowing she was alone in her house didn't stop her from looking around while the altered voice continued.

"Publicly announce your intention to resign from your position and name a male successor within the next forty-eight hours or this video will be sent to the chairman of the board then posted online. Do you want the world to see you like a black bitch in heat receiving stud service from the man paid to please you and to indulge your dirty whorish desires? We think not. Going to the authorities or consulting with your colleagues will result in the immediate exposure of your shameful nature, which violates the morals clause in your employment contract. You have until eleven a.m. Eastern Time on Monday to comply."

Complete silence. The screen blanked.

Slowly, Alexa lowered her tablet to the floor in front of her before her trembling hands could drop it.

She breathed in through her nose for five counts and out through her nose for five. Again. And again. Her eyes welled with furious tears, but she didn't cry. She refused to cry. She needed to plot a strategy. She needed to see Beck.

❧❦❧

Beckford Gallegas removed his welder's mask and set it on its stand on the long metal work table while he turned his head from side to side, then rolled his shoulders once his hands were free from holding the torch, the mask, and wearing his welder's gloves. He hooked the protective apron on one of the iron pegs hammered into the edge of the work table.

Seeing the finished metal sculpture pleased him greatly, but it wasn't the source of the spontaneous grin he felt stretching his scruffy face. His unexpected muse was. Alexa Davis Spencer fascinated him, challenged him, inspired him, pleased him. She often confused him. She always made understanding her worth his effort.

He'd almost passed up on the opportunity to meet her seven months ago. Financially precarious circumstances had forced him to accept the unsolicited offer from the exclusive LuxeLinks escort membership service that catered to a refined female clientele. Each member's liquid assets totaled at least fifty million dollars to qualify for an invitation to join. Escort candidates were exhaustively vetted through medical and psychological testing, criminal and credit background checks.

Beck made decent money as a tenured elementary school art teacher during the regular school year and as a freelance children's book illustrator, muralist, and mixed-media artist in his spare time. Not really much spare time between supporting his widowed mom stricken with ALS, and ensuring that his significantly younger twin sisters had money for college text books and supplies and everything their academic scholarships didn't cover as they completed their sophomore year.

The LuxeLinks director had said that his character and his finances made him the perfect candidate as a potential escort: his need to support his family. All the escorts were required to have college degrees or equivalent in life experience and a documented history of gainful employment in addition to three personal and three professional references. Their slogan was No fortune hunters. No gold diggers. And their rigorous selection process and mandatory confidentiality agreements honored that pledge.

LuxeLinks paid a monthly retainer for escorts to remain on-call to act as arm candy on evenings and weekends, or for longer assignments during his spring, summer, and winter school breaks. The contract specifically stated in bold underlined text highlighted in bright yellow that LuxeLinks facilitated introductions and platonic companionship, not sex. If consenting adults decided to engage in sexual acts, those were private decisions unrelated to LuxeLinks. The club, the members or the escorts could terminate the contract at will without prejudice. Beck had terminated his contract after his second companion assignment with Lex. When he met her for coffee the next day to tell her what he'd done, Lex had pulled out her cell and terminated her membership with a provocative smile on her face while he listened.

They had been monogamously committed to each other ever since that day six months earlier.

Each month since, the gallery that sold his work on consignment requested more and more of his newer works in his "Defiant" series. Paying the second mortgage and for full-time in-home nursing care for his mom no longer required him to subsidize his calorie intake by eating leftover cafeteria breakfast and lunch at school during the week to stretch their grocery budget as far as possible.

His twin sisters claimed that they sincerely preferred living at home and commuting rather than being on campus because doing so made the money from their part-time jobs go farther. If his finances kept improving, maybe he could afford to convert the half-bath in the basement into a luxurious full bath. Then Portia and Lindsey wouldn't need to share the one in the upstairs hall with their mom—or with him, too, whenever he spent the night. Their family home was his official address and the one on his driver's license, but he really lived here in his studio in a renovated warehouse in a blighted part of the city that had once been a thriving industrial district. The city had sold him the structure and its half-acre lot for the cost of a few thousand dollars in cash for back taxes owed by the previous owner. Its location offered plenty of space and peace and privacy. It was his sanctuary. Storage units and auto repair shops were his neighbors.

The chime of an old-fashioned doorbell rang

throughout the cavernous space just as his phone vibrated in his front pocket. He pulled it free as he walked toward the smaller door set into the cinderblock wall next to the double loading bay doors of corrugated steel.

>I'm @ your door.

He read Lex's text from the phone cupped in one palm while his other hand cranked the mechanism to retract the full-length bolt from its slot in the thick wall barring the solid steel door from swinging open.

"Lex—umph," he said as she propelled herself over the threshold and into his arms, which automatically closed around her. Both of their phones dropped to the polished cement floor.

"Hey now, hey, Lex, what's wrong?" he crooned, turning to kick the door closed while she trembled in his embrace. "Are you hurt, Lex? Lex?"

He pushed back to hold her at arm's length with his hands cupping her shoulders. His eyes started a visual inspection at the wild mane of dark waves falling from a zigzagged center part and stopping at the soft curve of her chin. Her dark eyes stared at him through a glossy sheen of unshed tears. Her smooth brown skin looked as lickable as ever, but there was the shadow of an uncharacteristically sallow undertone.

Beck released her shoulders in favor of claiming her hands to tug her toward the lounging area in the corner farthest from his designated work area. "Talk to me, Lex," he said when they were seated on the queen-sized day bed arranged between two leather recliners all facing a huge curved-screen television, the flashy new centerpiece of his impressive home entertainment media setup.

Her delectable breasts rose and fell with her sigh before she shrugged the vermillion tote off her shoulder and down off her arm. She reached in and pulled out her tablet and a black thumb drive.

"This was delivered to my house today, Beck."

Lex's body tightened up as if she were bracing herself to absorb a hit as she inserted the drive into its slot and held the screen so he could see.

Seeing the sunny blue skies, citrus trees, and entrance gate would have made him smile with fond memories of the most satisfying sex of his life, if Lex's trembling body were not so rigidly held beside him. As soon as he saw the familiar bedroom interior, his arm embraced her shoulders and pulled her into his side, tucking her more delicate frame against his larger, stronger body. After watching the first minute in real time, Beck fast-forwarded to the last image.

"Wait, Beck, there's a message for me," she said when he moved to lay the tablet on the nearest end table he'd crafted out of discarded glass and scrap metal struts.

"Alexa Davis Spencer, CEO of Universal Tapestry Group, a Fortune One Hundred company, publicly announce your intention to resign from your position and name a male successor within the next forty-eight hours or this video will be sent to the chairman of the board, then posted online…

"You have until eleven a.m. Eastern Time Monday to comply."

He let her remove the tablet from his clutching grip and place it on the end table while he marveled at his ability to feel sexually aroused and thoroughly appalled at the same time.

Lex hadn't looked him in the eye since she'd started the video playback.

Beck shifted, pushing toward Lex until gravity had them lying across the day bed with Lex flat on her back. He hovered above her in a low plank pushup. "Tell me how you want us to fight this, Lex."

఼఼

Meeting his fierce dark gaze directly was very difficult—almost as difficult as inhaling deeply to speak the words she needed to say next.

"Beck, I can't give in to these people. First, because it's just wrong. Second, there's no guarantee that they won't release the video anyway." She took a deep breath that nudged her breasts against his muscular chest. "I don't want your reputation to get smeared with mine." Looking deeply into his eyes, Lex very softly said, "I think we should take a break until this is resolved."

Beck was already shaking his head. "No, Lex," he grumbled. "Not just no, but hell, no, Lex," he whispered before his mouth claimed her parted lips.

He dropped his weight upon her from chest to crotch, settling into the cradle of her splayed thighs and dry humping her as if they were horny virgin teenagers.

Between carnal kisses, he asked, "Do you know why that video got you soaking wet?" His tongue licked deeply into her open mouth while he angled his hips to grind his hard penis covered in worn denim against her mons, her clitoris, and her vulva. He raised his head. "Do you?" he rasped.

"Yes," she moaned, using her double-fisted grip on his thick hair to drag his mouth back down to her lips.

He used his tongue to fill her, to stroke her, to invade her senses through penetrating her mouth while his strong hands wrestled with her clothing until the rip of tearing threads and rending fabric preceded the rush of air between her splayed thighs.

Beck looked up from her drenched folds, framed in shredded material, to hold her motionless in his feral gaze.

"You're primed to go off with one stroke, aren't you?" he asked as he unbuckled his belt, loosened the top button of his waistband, then unzipped his fly to push his jeans and briefs down until his erection and sac spilled free. "Do you want me?" he asked, firmly gripping the base of his erection in one hand and sliding forward to trace the tip up and down her labia before prodding her stiffly protruding clitoris.

They both cried out at the jolt of the tip to tip connection.

"Do you want me, Lex?"

Her hands reached between her legs to guide him into her vagina. "Yes, Beck, I want you now, tomorrow, always." She screamed the last word as he plunged forward and continued thrusting until her voice was reduced to hoarse whispers of demand.

Finally, the rushing warmth of his orgasm flooded her, and his full weight collapsed upon her with a deep, sighing groan.

☙❧

Soft cursing accompanied gentle tugging on her lower body. When Alexa opened her eyes, she saw that Beck was all tucked away and covered up again and had worked the remnants of her destroyed leggings down to her knees, but he seemed stumped about how to get them over her calves pressed flat against the mattress without waking her.

"I'm awake," she said, drawing his frowning gaze from the bunched up leggings to her face.

He smiled. "Good." He jerked once, and the leggings rolled down her calves, over her ankles and off her bare feet. He must have removed her leather ballet flats.

She couldn't remember kicking them off.

Beck reached toward the floor and straightened up with a large metal bowl in one hand. With the other he grabbed one of her ankles and pulled, dragging her closer, sliding her bare bottom across quilted cotton and making her fitted knit shirt ride up until she was exposed from plain black cotton bra to painted toes.

Beck's eyelids drooped, and his nostrils flared, suggesting the imminent start of another round of debauchery. Instead, he dipped his hands into the metal bowl to squeeze the excess water from a wash cloth, which he used to clean gently across her inner thighs and at the apex between her legs.

"Here, Lex." He reached behind his back and offered her one of his white dress shirts after he rubbed his hands dry on his jeans. "Lindsey and Portia have some clothes here if you want to borrow some pants or a skirt to wear home," he spoke softly while his eyes tracked her every movement as she tugged her shirt down to her waist, then shrugged into his shirt and buttoned the bottom four buttons. She rolled each sleeve cuff several times until her wrists and forearms remained visible.

His relaxed pose didn't fool her. Beck was ready to fight.

"Loan me one of your solid neckties to use as a belt, and I'll just wear this as a shirt dress."

CHAPTER 3

Beck watched the woman he loved finger-comb her thick hair while she waited for him to respond when all he wanted to do was to drag her astride his lap and fuck her until she acknowledged that they were a permanent, for better or for worse, couple. No breaks. No timeouts. No handling things on her own to protect him. Their age difference didn't give her the right to treat him like a child. She wasn't old enough to be his mother.

"Lex, you know that I go to flea markets, yard sales, Dumpster diving, and junkyards to find materials and interesting objects to integrate into my art," he said, pulling on the chain around his neck strung with his father's military identification tags.

Lex stopped fussing with the arrangement of her

clothes to step closer, standing between his spread legs while Beck looped the chain over his head to unfasten it and remove the item he had added to it last week.

"Its shape caught my attention when I saw it among the debris in the junkyard last week. It was black and green, dull from oxidation and tarnish, but I liked its shape and its balance. Took it to a jeweler who's bought a few of my pieces over the years and asked him to clean it up."

The ring lay in the palm of his hand.

"It's a perfectly round, cultured pearl surrounded by brilliant round diamonds. The entire configuration is supported by a gallery of intricately woven, thin sterling silver strands to create a basket that's been melded at the base into the simple sterling silver band. There's no maker's mark or inscription or insignia of any kind beyond the designation of silver content, but the jeweler believes its materials, form, technique and craftsmanship date it somewhere between the mid to late 1800s."

Still seated, Beck pulled Lex closer with his free hand at her waist. They were almost nose to nose.

"I've loved you for months now, Lex. Please marry me."

⌘

So many doubts bubbled up to the surface of her thoughts. Issues they had discussed months earlier swirled into a discordant chorus of indecision. She was eleven years older than Beck. She didn't want to give birth to children or adopt or foster parent. She adored her nieces and nephews and mentored high school and college interns at work because she enjoyed spending time with smart, ambitious young people and she owed it to her mentors to do for others what they had done for her as a UTG intern years ago.

Beck's vasectomy was more than five years old, so she believed his claims that being more of a father to his twin sisters than a big brother, plus spending most weekdays with hundreds of elementary school kids left him grateful for a private life that didn't include conventional parenthood.

Beck was a grown man who knew his own mind. He was asking her to marry him because he wanted her to marry him. She wanted the same.

"Yes, Beck, I've loved you for months, too" She leaned into him and pressed a kiss to his lips. "Yes, I'll marry you."

He smiled against her mouth as he slid the ring onto her finger. It fit just right.

ℰↄℰↄ

An hour later, after using a new prepaid cell phone to call the chairman of the Universal Tapestry Group Board and to give the LuxeLinks director a heads-up, Alexa and

Beck were on their way to the airport to fill two vacant seats on a private charter flight to Las Vegas.

⌘⌘⌘

Against both families' strenuously voiced objections during an earlier Sunday afternoon conference call, only Alexa stood at the microphone with Beckford's vibrant presence at her back. The UTG image consultant had signed off on Beck's wardrobe choices of his father's distressed cognac leather racing jacket over an untucked, faded black T-shirt with *Artists make the world more beautiful* hugged across his torso in faint white script. Relaxed fit, straight-legged jeans in midnight blue slouched across the tops of his battered dark gray, paint-splattered steel-toed construction boots.

The image consultant had asked Beck, "What message do you want your clothes to send?"

"That I'm a sensitive artist who will kick the ass of anyone who threatens Alexa or me or anyone we love."

The image consultant's glance had swept over Beck from his thick, dark, wavy hair brushed straight back from his widow's peak, across two-plus days of beard scruff, down the length of his neck and chest and body to his widely spread feet. "Mission accomplished," she'd said.

After spritzing Alexa's face with a finishing mist to set her makeup and eliminate any unflattering shine, the consultant had taken a final three-sixty look at her client from her beautifully defined natural waves of thick, dark hair, modest pearl studs in her ears, minimal cosmetics on her face. The sleeveless V-neck sheath in a pattern of pale watercolors edged in thin black piping at the seams ended an inch below her knees. It was one of the garments hastily purchased at a high-end fair trade goods boutique en route to the airport yesterday before catching their Vegas flight.

Sky high heels displayed her toned legs and hydrated brown skin.

Alexa felt prepared and strong. She felt ready, and the consultant's nod indicated that the other woman agreed.

"Call me if your man has a single brother or cousin or uncle or best friend, Alexa!" she'd whispered before leaving them in the green room a few minutes before the scheduled start time for the press conference in the adjacent UTG headquarters press room.

Now, with eighteen hours until the extortionists' deadline, Alexa's gaze scanned the crowd of fidgeting business journalists and smiled.

"Thank you all for coming in on a Sunday evening on such last-minute notice."

"Is Universal Tapestry Group building another solar-powered textile factory in a contested location?" someone shouted from the back of the crowded room.

"A new micro-to-macro financing coalition?"

"More book exchanges?"

"Leadership academies?"

"Indigenous people's trade alliances?"

Alexa shook her head and waved in a non-verbal command for silence.

"Our programs are all thriving and spurring development from one motivated individual up to grassroots and beyond." She always managed to work the slogan for their philanthropic division into every business speech. Sometimes her colleagues teased her about making it into a drinking game.

"No, we're gathered here today to announce my very recent marriage to the artist, Beckford Gallegas."

Alexa caught a whiff of her new husband's heady scent and felt the heat of his nearness along the back of her body from head to heels. "Over the past several months many of you have seen us together at professional and social gatherings as friends. Some of you know that we met through an invitation-only introduction club.

"Someone wants to use that fact to force me to resign as CEO of UTG and name my successor. By refusing to do so, anonymous extortionists have threatened to release an illegally recorded video of my husband and me during intimate moments in a private vacation residence.

"The chairman and the board voted unanimously to support my decision. They will continue to endorse my leadership as long as UTG's growth continues under my command.

"Now I'll take questions."

"How were you contacted, Ms. Spencer, or are you Mrs. Gallegas now?"

"A thumb drive sent via US Mail," Alexa said, then smiled. "I remain myself as Ms. Spencer, but I'll answer to Mrs. Gallegas if Beckford's mom isn't nearby."

"Which authorities are investigating?"

"The FBI, the Post Master General, and the SEC. Extortion is a Federal crime, and they used the US Mail to do it. The authorities suspect this is a ploy to exploit personal vulnerabilities for the purpose of corporate espionage. UTG is a publicly traded stock. Manipulating me equates to manipulating the company, and ultimately, the market." She and Beck had made an abridged copy of the video for the investigators to watch and to keep despite being pressured to surrender the full-length original.

Alexa answered all of the journalists' questions and ignored thinly veiled references to her being a cougar, or a sugar mama, without pause until someone in the front row asked, "How do you know that your new husband hasn't done this to coerce you into a marriage that instantly ups his public profile and his private net worth?"

In the absolute silence of shock and anticipation, she said, "Beck, I'll ask you to answer that."

When she moved to step aside, his right arm hooked around her waist as he leaned down and to the left to speak into the stick microphone. His left hand rested on the edge of the podium in clear view for everyone in the room to see his shiny platinum wedding band.

"Secretly recording people without their knowledge or consent is a cowardly act committed by ball-less, impotent, creeper peepers without honor or courage.

"There's nothing shameful about anything Alexa and I were doing with each other in that video, but it was sacred. It was private time for us to deepen our connection as a couple. And some anonymous smucks violated our privacy with malicious intent. If that video is released, everyone will see that my wife is hotter than fire and people will understand why I used this situation to convince her to elope to Vegas as quickly as possible yesterday rather than waiting.

"Let me state the obvious for the public record that Alexa is more than smart enough and strong enough to protect herself and the company, but I will not allow threats against my wife to go unchallenged."

Alexa didn't think Beck realized how much his right arm had tightened around her waist with his splayed fingers and broad palm pulling her closer against his bigger body.

She reached forward with her left hand to cover his left hand where his fingers were digging into the edge of the podium. Light bounced off the shiny platinum of their matching simple wedding bands and the luminescent pearl and diamonds of her engagement ring.

"Alexa has given me her whole self and her sacred pledge to build a life with me. With that, she's made me the richest man in the world. When the authorities catch the gut-less smucks behind this failed attempt to bully Alexa out of the CEO position she's earned through dragging UTG from the edge of bankruptcy and successfully taking it public, the world will know I'm not guilty. For now, Alexa loves me and trusts me, and her opinion is the only one that matters to me."

Releasing his tight grip on the podium, he took a short step backward and used his right arm around Alexa's waist to shift her directly in front of his body, making it easier for her to speak into the microphone again. The warm strength of his right hand stayed at her waist.

"Thank you again for coming. This concludes the press conference. Goodnight."

Alexa turned and stepped toward the edge of the platform. She felt the drag of Beck's right hand across the side of her waist, down her hip and away from her body while her left hand reached back until his long, rough fingers snagged hers as they stepped off the small stage and exited the room amidst a barrage of shouted questions and camera clicks and some flashes.

∽∾∽

"You and Alexa were breaking news tonight, Beckford!" Portia squealed as he and Lex entered the crowded living room in his family's home. Since the three minutes younger twin seldom felt the need to speak unless she was asked a direct question, Beck knew she was really impressed by their sudden notoriety.

Alexa's parents, Matthew and Luccia Spencer, popped up from their seats on the doily-dotted sofa near the archway into the dining room with a speed and agility that belied their senior citizen status.

Matthew, Jr. and his wife Charlotte approached from standing in the far corner of the room with their tween sons, Charles and James.

After multiple rounds of handshakes, hugs and kisses, and a lovingly stern command from Beck's mom's computer-generated voice for everyone to have a seat, Luccia said to Alexa, "Your sisters made me promise to conference call them once you arrived, sweetheart." She looked down at her phone as she continued. "You know Marie, and Davida and her wife, Elaine, will pitch a fit if they miss one word."

A few minutes later all three women were joining in the conversation.

"One anchor called you the CEO Beauty and Her Fierce Beast. I think she was drooling," Marie said, making no attempt to disguise her amusement.

"I know!" Davida chimed in. "Even I got a little tingly, Beckford, when I saw that final warning glare you swept over the press as you let Alexa drag you out of the room. You looked ticked off and ready to rumble."

"Hey, no flirting with our new brother-in-law, baby,"

projected faintly into the living room in the alto pitch of Elaine's voice as if she was not very close to her wife's phone.

"Appreciating from afar is not cheating, E.," Davida said.

Everyone laughed, except the young boys, whose eyes and attention were glued to their phones.

The conference call ended with vague references to planning a second ceremony at Alexa's dad's and brother's church and an official wedding reception, then with overlapping I love yous, which led Matthew, Jr. to say privately to Alexa, "Really proud of you, Bigger Sister. Someone tried to punk you, and you didn't flinch," as he hugged her in preparation for his family's departure.

"Whoever they are might still post the video just for spite, M.J."

He shook his head. "Probably not, Al. Your husband labeled that as a smuck move. Beckford also called you hotter than fire, so now everyone's dying to see you in action. Check. Mate. Game over for the extortionists."

"I hope you're right."

☙❧

"You said she would comply."

The older man shrugged. "Her father and brother are the most senior ministers of a Christian mega church. She's CEO of a company that conducts more than thirty percent of its business with Islamic countries. She should have resigned for fear of tanking UTG's stock value and ruining her professional credibility."

He and the younger man shared a look.

"No one respects or trusts a woman who thinks with her twat," they said in unison.

The younger man said, "Maybe if she had been sucking his dick or on her hands and knees while he was sodomizing her—or if the camera had caught all of their bedroom activity during the entire weekend instead of malfunctioning that first night, the threat of posting the video would have been effective against her." Then he asked, "Will you release the video anyway?"

The older man snorted a negative huff. "Can't, now that the young stud she's married to all but dared me to and has everyone thinking 'sleazy creeper peeper and smuck' if I do. Did you see the look on his face when he called his wife hotter than fire? That phrase is already trending worldwide. So no, as much as I'd personally enjoy having the whole world see prim and proper Alexa Davis Spencer taking it deep like a professionally trained working girl, it's time to move on to the next target with a different approach.

"I've destroyed the Spencer video. I refuse to give the salacious masses what they so desperately crave. We'll need to discredit the LuxeLinks Club members in other ways. Having all those rich, powerful hetero and QUILTBAG women dictating terms and demanding that their escorts meet such high requirements is not the natural order of traditional civilized society. It's a rebellion that needs to be crushed before the grand opening of their private beach club for unnaturally powerful women."

CHAPTER 4

Margeaux Carr Hirsch smiled through her second viewing of Alexa's press conference. Julianna and Chloe had gone back to their respective apartments in their jointly owned renovated Harlem brownstone after their brainstorming session about who was targeting LuxeLinks members.

None of the attempts had been successful. Yet. The repeated attempts and escalating menace of each one were cause for serious concern. First, "I know you pay to play." emails to a couple of members, then still photos of innocent meetings at coffee houses and cocktail parties mailed to two other members as they conversed with their chosen escorts. No explicit threats or demands included in any of those four incidents. The jump from that to this near-miss with Alexa alarmed Margeaux and her sisters.

They needed to get proactive to protect themselves and their LuxeLinks Club membership from these unknown adversaries who had probably bribed the Seaside Enclave housekeeper in charge of preparing Alexa and Beckford's cottage. The woman had not reported for work at the Florida resort since the week after the couple's stay.

The grand opening of their private LuxeLinks Beach Club in Oyster Glen Cove, Maryland was two months away. Finishing touches on the bayside dock, boat slips, and half-mile of sugar sand beach along the Atlantic Ocean were scheduled for completion at the end of next month for final code compliance inspections along with the central structure, guest cottages, and PWGA golf course.

Opening their own private resort would allow LuxeLinks to guarantee their members' privacy and security because the property was isolated and their hiring process for all staff included deep background checks that rivaled what was required for top security clearance at the Pentagon.

She was surprised Uncle J. Lo hadn't called. Jaime Lowenthal remained as protective of the Hirsch sisters now as if they were still the same scared little girls he'd first met 20 years ago when he'd requested a three-dollar retainer in exchange for protecting their financial interests.

Margeaux picked up the handset on her desk phone and dialed his home number.

☙❧

Beck easily swung Alexa up into his arms after he unlocked the door to his warehouse studio. He stared down into her eyes as their bodies crossed the threshold.

"Yesterday, you left here as my intended, Lex. Tonight, you're my bride."

He hip-checked the door closed, then leaned his back against it before letting her legs swing free to the floor and pulling her to stand between his spread legs. Standing chest to breasts, he laid his lips on her mouth while his hands at her waist lifted her to the tips of her toes in her sky high heels.

His mouth on hers, his chest against her breasts, and the prod of his erection in her stomach ratcheted up her desire to make love with him now that the weight of her worries about the press conference was gone.

She moaned and tilted her chin when his mouth drifted to her cheek and down the side of her neck. She felt one of his hands leave her waist while his torso twisted slightly before she heard the lock bar slide into place across the door.

In the next instant, she was airborne as Beck swung her into his arms again and carried her through the dark space filled with the looming shadows of his works in progress and newly finished pieces.

His heavy tread up the open fretwork metal stairs to his sleeping loft echoed.

Alexa kissed his neck and his chest, wherever she could reach with her arms looped around his neck for leverage and security, drowning her senses in his taste and his touch, his scent and his strength. At the top of the stairs, the layout of the generous loft space was softly illuminated by the glow of the exterior security lights affixed to each upper corner of his building. A previous owner had filled in the adjustable ventilation grate near the roof line with two rows of block glass.

"Do you want me to lower the shades?" Beck asked as he lowered her feet to stand on the plank floor that had been repurposed from a decommissioned barn. He looked toward the highboy chest where the remote that controlled the automatic window coverings was stored in its designated cubby.

She shook her head. "No, I want to see you," she said, shrugging out of her black silk baseball jacket with a pastel watercolor lining. She let it drop to the floor and stepped forward into his body to reach up and push his leather jacket off his shoulders.

When his arms embraced her, she laid her cheek to his chest and hugged him around his waist. The impression of his dad's military I.D. tags pressed her temple through the soft cotton of his T-shirt. She felt his hand tug the tab high between her shoulder blades and heard and felt the zipper descend.

His fingers lightly traced the skin he'd exposed. "I kept staring at this smooth patch of skin just below the nape of your neck, and I wanted to lick it," he whispered, "then bite it."

His other hand coasted lower, tugging up the hem of her dress to expose her skin and lingerie. He palmed her butt and squeezed. The friction of his toughened skin sliding over the smooth silk of her plain white bikini panties made her shiver.

"I wanted to lift your skirt, bend you over that podium, spread your legs—" He stepped back to work her unzipped dress off her shoulders, down her arms and over her hands until the fitted frock draped her hips, leaving her upper body in only a sheer, plunging lacy white bra to accent her nakedness. His glittering eyes devoured her.

"While you were standing tall and strong, talking smart, and looking like the embodiment of sophisticated command, Lex, I was so proud of you. I was thanking God for the privilege of being your man. And I couldn't wait to see you like this again."

Beck reached up and over to pull his t-shirt up and off before letting it drop to the floor.

His broad shoulders and muscular arms perfectly framed the depth of his chest as it tapered to his ribcage, then narrowed to his tight waist belted in black leather with silver grommets running its length. The glint from the loop of thin metal chain and two rectangular tags winked in the subdued lighting, tugging her gaze back up to his chest.

Alexa grabbed his belt buckle and loosened it by feel

as she looked up higher into his fierce gaze. "Being your woman, Beck. Having you with me today made me feel invincible because no matter what might happen, you love me as much as I love you." She nudged aside the dangling ends of his unfastened belt while she unbuttoned and unzipped his jeans, then she slid one hand into his briefs.

"I need you, Beck."

His abdominal muscles rolled against the back of her hand.

⁂

Beck panted to avoid ejaculating all over her delicate hand, which tantalized with just her soft touch. She wasn't even squeezing. If he were to put his hands on her right now, her clothes wouldn't survive. He already owed her a pair of leggings.

"Will you strip for me, Lex?"

⁂

Alexa felt the hard thumping pulse in his erection echo the rhythm of his heavy panting breath.

"Yes." She slid her hand free of his jeans and stepped backward. "After you strip for me, Beck."

The flare of surprise that flashed in his eyes made her smile as she inched backward, hopping up to sit on the edge of his king-sized bed set atop the high platform Beck had constructed from scrap metal and reclaimed wood.

She watched his eyes move from her anticipatory grin to her lips to her breasts before his gaze dropped to track the movement of her legs as she crossed them at her knees, which halted the swinging motion of her feet.

"Fast of slow, Lex?"

She leaned back on her elbows without breaking eye contact. "Your choice, Beck."

He laughed.

Beck turned sideways and folded over at the waist, the jingle of his loose belt and pocket change his only music. She watched him pull up one pants leg to unlace his boot before twisting slightly to repeat those moves on the other side.

For Alexa, it seemed as if it took forever for him to rise again to his full height. He stared directly into her eyes while he heeled off one boot, then the other and kicked them aside before turning his beautifully defined back to her, but keeping his gaze locked with hers until he was looking at her over his shoulder.

His hands rested loosely near the waistband of his jeans. With a flick of his wrist, his belt snaked free of all the denim loops with a jangling swoosh and clanked to the floor.

Now, in addition to the brand name on the elastic band of his briefs, she could see the firm upper curve of his very fine butt. Alexa laughed when he shook it from side to side.

"Tease," she whispered.

His amused gaze stroked over her from head to shoes in her provocative pose. "Takes one to know one, Lex."

Instead of dropping his jeans, Beck folded over at the waist again, mooning her while he tugged off his socks, revealing his strong, square feet.

This time when he stood up, Beck didn't look at her over his shoulder. He tucked his fingers into the waistband of his jeans and pushed, slowly revealing more of his utterly delectable glutes wrapped in pale gray cotton. Once the denim cleared his hard, muscular thighs, he let the pants drop to his ankles before he kicked free of them.

He turned his head to catch her gaze with his. "You ready, Lex? You're licking your lips like you see something you want." His body slowly rotated toward her. "You're gasping for breath. Your licorice drop nipples are poking the lace of your bra."

When he completed the turn, the prominent bulge between his spread legs captured her entire visual focus.

He stepped one long stride forward, then another. The third step brought him within touching proximity.

"Is this what you want, Lex?" he asked, hooking his thumbs into the sides of his briefs. His deep inhalation lifted his pectorals. "Your scent tells me you do."

He pulled the elastic waistband down until his glistening erection and sac were free, then he stopped, leaving his genitalia balanced along the stretchy material as if it were a sling. He let his hands dangle freely at his sides.

"Take what you want, Lex. Finish stripping me bare."

Alexa barely controlled her impulse to jump him. She wanted to ravage him. Instead, she uncrossed her legs. She spread them as much as the hiked up hem of her dress allowed. It gave her enough range of motion to maneuver the tip of one spiked heel under the leg band at his hip. She carefully executed the same move with her other heel on his other side, bending her knees and drawing them toward her chest to bring him closer.

"All this just for me, Beck. I'm flattered."

Licking her lips after she said it must have been one tease too many because her heels popped free when Beck jerked his briefs down and off before he grabbed her waist and flipped her onto her stomach.

"Here's your flattery, Lex," he rasped against her ear as his hands pulled one of her legs straight down to the floor and arranged her other leg bent at the knee with her thigh propped against the edge of the mattress.

Cool air across her thighs and hips made her shiver when Beck shoved the material of her dress higher up around her waist. There was the sound of tearing fabric accompanied by feeling the drag of silk and fibers on her skin before her low-cut bikini briefs disappeared, baring her butt and her legs of any coverage other than her spiked heels and the muscular blanket of his hot body.

The abrupt addition of his heavy weight against her

from shoulders to thighs crushed her upper body between the soft, silky duvet and his fragrant hard body.

"This is what I was thinking while you were standing firm in the face of adversity, Lex."

His erection trailed wetness down the cleft of her buttocks.

"I was wishing we were somewhere private so I could do this."

That was her only warning before he gathered his momentum on a deep breath that rubbed nearly three days of beard growth against the side of her face and ended on a hard thrust that shoved her off her only stabilized foot. Metal chain and tags lightly scraped her spine.

Beyond grunts and cries and whispered profanities, neither of them spoke another coherent word while, despite being inside the cage of Beck's arms, Alexa got her hands under her shoulders with her palms braced flat against the mattress as the clenching muscles of her sex yielded way to accept each hard stroke from tip to root again, and again.

The power behind each thrust slapped her flesh with a titillating sting heightened by the sound of taut, sweaty naked flesh hitting softer, sweaty naked flesh.

Her elevated feet gave her no leverage for pushing back to meet him measure for measure. She was obliged to lie face-down under his weight and take it hard and long as he drilled her and claimed her and worked her mons and clitoris against the edge of the mattress.

Beck pushed balls-deep, then held still for a moment before rocking his hips.

"Does this help, Lex?"

A sobbing cry was her only reply. She let her head hang as she panted, then screamed a high-pitched scream when Beck lifted and bent her straight leg to mirror the other.

She could move now. And she did, angling forward to raise her hips to make space for her to reach one hand back between her legs to brush her fingertips over her clitoris, launching her body into orgasm as she frantically pumped her butt.

Beck took the hint and started slam stroking nearly all the way out, then all the way in, dragging and pushing her squeezing muscles to milk him harder until he filled her with the hot, wet rush of his orgasm.

She felt his tongue lick the patch of skin at the top of her spine before he opened his mouth wider and nibbled.

⁂

Alexa tried to slip out of bed without waking her new husband, but his arms tightened around her waist.

"Time's it, Lex?"

She turned in his embrace. "Early," she whispered, hoping to lull him back to sleep. "I need to check the opening markets. Your alarm's set for six-thirty. I'll call you during your lunch break." She kissed his lips as she reached behind her back to unlace his fingers. "Love you, Beck," she said, rolling away to move through a brief yoga flow before going out to face the consequences of her actions.

CHAPTER 5

UTG stock was up seven percent when the Australian markets opened. The Asian-Pacific markets continued the positive trend. In the odd logic of the international finance universe, the attempt to force Alexa to resign, and her refusal, had upped the perception of her influence and increased the valuation of her market power and that of UTG by association.

Everyone was all smiles when Alexa entered the main conference room at UTG headquarters where the voting members of the board were gathered physically, virtually, and by proxy to conduct this hastily scheduled strategy session.

"Our stock prices are up in all the markets and the average social media score for all mentions of Alexa Davis Spencer, Beckford Gallegas, UTG, hotter than fire, or any of his other catchy phrases is eighty-nine percent positive." The public relations liaison practically bubbled in her seat.

"All variations of your dress sold out from the designer's site in twenty minutes. Knock-offs from other stores in an hour. Similar sales frenzy with your shoes and Beck's t-shirt. Unconditional support from the major black political action associations. Most feminist groups are publicly endorsing you for standing up to slut-shaming. Although some representatives of those same groups are displeased that you felt the need to get married and have a man defend your honor."

Alexa stared at the woman and silently counted to three before she said, "It's his honor, too."

The PR liaison nodded and waved away the issue.

"The UTG site has crashed twice with the spike in visitor volume. Reception drafted some interns to help answer phones and reply to e-mails. Security has been politely declining access to a steady stream of paparazzi and Looky Lous.

"We sent two retired police officers to the Gallegas home. One for the front and the other for the back."

Alexa was disappointed in herself for not thinking to protect Beck's mother and sisters. Alexa's parents also lived in a gated community. Her younger sister Marie was currently directing an indie film on location in West Sussex, England with her three kids along for cultural exposure. Her other younger sister Davida and her wife

Elaine lived on the other side of the country in San Francisco, and their baby brother, Matt, Jr.'s, family resided in an impenetrable fortress designed by their mother. Her family was safe.

Where else were they vulnerable?

ঙঙ

"Mr. Beckford."

Caller I.D. on the hands-free system in his truck had announced the caller as Lisa Newman, his mom's full-time nurse on weekdays, so he'd expected to hear her soft southern twang. He hadn't expected it to vibrate with anxiety.

He'd given up trying to get her to drop the mister from his name a long time ago.

"The house phone has been ringing non-stop since dawn. I finally just unplugged it once the voice mailbox was full. The nice retired policemen from your wife's company made the reporters go away. Portia and Lindsey got permission from their professors to e-mail their assignments and watch the streaming of today's classes so they can stay home with Mrs. Gallegas today."

"Thank you so much, Lisa. Is everything else good?"

There was a long pause during which only the soft susurrus of an open connection let him know that the call hadn't ended.

"One of the callers offered me a lot of money if I

would answer some very personal questions about you and your family and take pictures of your bedroom, Mr. Beckford, and I was so tempted."

Still driving, Beck looked right, signaled, and pulled over to the curb about two miles from the public elementary school where he had been working for the past eight years.

"Thank you for telling me that, Lisa. Thank you for your loyalty to my family."

He heard sniffles.

"I just hate that I felt tempted, Mr. Beckford."

"Here's what we're going to do, Lisa. Can you stay with my mom and sisters until I get there around four-thirty?"

"Yes."

"Thank you, Lisa. I'm going to cancel the night nurse who usually arrives by four. Our current situation means we need to circle the wagons."

He remembered her never married, no kids status. "Would you consider a promotion to live-in house manager, Lisa? We need someone trustworthy to supervise the nurses who will care for my mom to make sure they respect her as a person, not just a patient."

Beck started juggling figures in his head. He owned his warehouse studio free and clear, just utilities, maintenance, insurance, and annual property taxes. His four-year-old truck that he'd bought used after putting more than three hundred thousand miles on his dad's old truck was already paid off. Seven more years on the second mortgage on his family's home was his largest monthly expenditure after healthcare premiums, but it wasn't an onerous financial burden, and neither was the twins' college books and supplies money.

"If Mrs. Gallegas and Portia and Lindsey want me to live in, I will, Mr. Beckford."

"Great, Lisa. We'll talk terms this evening."

Beck took care of cancelling the night nurse before he resumed his commute to work.

Seeing the news vans and reporters lining the normally quiet residential street that dead-ended at the school was an unpleasant surprise. His full-sized crew cab pickup truck had tinted windows. No one pointed or tried to follow when he rode past them, which led him to believe that they hadn't yet figured out that his truck and warehouse were registered as the property of Team Port Linds, LLC.

"Most of them were already here when I arrived," his principal said as Beck signed in.

"Must be a very slow news cycle," Beck said on his way out of the office.

༺༻

"Smuck!"

"Am not, you ball-less peeper creep!"

Well, that answered Beck's question about whether

or not any of his students had seen the press conference video.

He waded into the fray.

Standing between two second graders who alternated between being mortal enemies and best buddies, according to the mysteries of their own personal circadian rhythm of interaction, Beck looked down into one scowling dark brown face and one scowling pale brown face, both missing their two front teeth.

"First, no fighting. That's not the first choice of civilized humans for conflict resolution. Agreed?"

Both boys blinked up at him.

"Yes, Mr. Gallegas."

"Go sit on the contemplation bench until the end of recess."

After sharing a quick glance, both boys ducked their heads and kicked at the grass with their scuffed sneakers.

"Yes, Mr. Gallegas."

Beck shook his head as he watched them chase each other to the bench, where they argued about who would sit where until they settled into place when they noticed that Beck was watching.

"Oh, I see. It takes a big beast to tame the little beasts, Mr. Gallegas."

Beck groaned softly and turned. "Not you, too, Suzanna. Everyone has been amusing themselves all day at my expense."

"Well, boo-hoo for you, Beckford, newly married to

a brilliant, gorgeous, wealthy corporate power player who loves you so much that her eyes sparkle when she says your name." The pretty young second grade teacher was a newlywed herself. "I'm happily married to my own broody protector, so your whole don't fuck—" Her voiced dropped to almost nothing in volume. He read the profane word from her lips before she resumed speaking in her normal tones. "—with me or mine vibe last night rang true for me. I totally understand why women are lusting after you and lamenting your happily married status.

"Enjoy your time in the spotlight, Beckford. Next week will be someone else's turn." She shoulder-bumped him before stepping away to line up her students to take them inside.

Beck pulled his vibrating phone out of his front pocket as he walked the perimeter of the playground to scan for any stragglers.

"Hi, Lex."

"Hi, Beck. I've got about one minute before my next meeting. Where are we meeting up tonight?"

"My mom's. There's lots to discuss."

"Okay. I'll call if I won't get there by five. So far, the higher stock prices and mostly positive press have saved me from being reprimanded."

"For what? You did nothing wrong, and you've earned their support with your job performance. See you tonight. Love you, Lex."

"Bye. Love you, too, Fierce Beast."

He chuffed in surprise, mostly amused as the call ended.

❧

Beck had no clue about how or when he'd lost control of this family meeting.

"We have already decided, Beck*ford*." Lindsey said his name with the heavy emphasis on the last syllable expressing her impatience and displeasure with him the same way she had been saying it since she'd learned to talk. "If Miss Newman agrees to live in, Portia and I can stay with mom on evenings and weekends. Portia waits tables on Saturdays. I wait tables on Sundays."

Beck shook his head. "You need time to study, go out with friends or just daydream about what you want your life to be."

Lindsey scowled at him. "Beckford, when you were our age, you were working your way through college, helping us with our homework every night, helping us earn our scout badges, taking us to school, and chaperoning our field trips because Mom couldn't and Dad worked all the time except Sundays. You worked summer school and a weekend job to pay for our Quinceañera

"We know you want us to have the carefree college experience you didn't have, but we're old enough to carry our share of the family responsibilities."

Lindsey did all the convincing as usual while Portia stood shoulder to shoulder with her three-minutes-older twin and stared him down. Where had the time gone? It felt like only yesterday that he had been sneaking into their rooms to slide dollar bills from the tooth fairy under their pillows. Now they stood before him as these intelligent, honorable, strikingly beautiful young women.

Seated next to him, Alexa stroked his thigh with the palm of her hand. "May I offer a compromise?" she asked then waited for Lisa to push his mom's motorized wheelchair closer.

The twins shared a side chair while Lisa perched on the arm of the sofa.

"Mrs. Gallegas, as the newest member of your family, may I offer you a gift in appreciation for this honorable man you and your husband raised?"

His mom blinked once for yes. She saved the computer-generated voice for longer responses.

Alexa's grip briefly tightened on Beck's thigh. "Thank you," she said to his mom before she turned to face him. "Beck, the gift I want to give to my new family is overnight and weekend nursing—No, Beck, let me finish," she said when he shook his head and opened his mouth.

"What's the use of having money if I can't use it for the benefit of people we love, Beck?" To the group, Alexa said, "With Miss Newman as a live-in house manager, her nursing credentials make her the perfect supervisor for the two nurses we'll hire to work exclusively for Mrs. Gallegas after they're thoroughly vetted and sign confidentiality contracts. A rotation gives everybody regular down time, coverage for holidays and vacations while Mrs. Gallegas remains safe and comfortable in her home with more flexibility for arranging excursions." Alexa made eye contact with his mom again. "Does that sound good to you?"

His mom's lips twitched, then she blinked once. Her computer-generated voice said, "Let's talk details while we eat."

CHAPTER 6

At the guard shack in front of the imposing entrance to her gated community, Alexa powered down her window.

"Good evening, Jack, no more paparazzi?" Her retired neighbor had texted updates to Alexa throughout the day.

"Hi, Ms. Spencer, the security chief threatened to call the police if they kept loitering. Plus, I think they heard you'd been spotted somewhere else, so they all vacated the premises."

Alexa nodded. "Good," she said before leaning her head out of her car window and pointing behind her. "See that truck right behind me, Jack?"

"Yes, Ms. Spencer."

"It belongs to my new husband, Beckford Gallegas.

Please switch his name, vehicle description, and tag number from the frequent visitors list to the permanent resident list. Okay?"

The guard nodded. "Sure thing, Ms. Spencer. Congratulations! I'll update his status in the system as soon as the gate closes behind his truck. Could you please e-mail the security chief that you made the request? He likes a clear document trail before he authorizes a new remote."

Alexa agreed. She asked Jack about his start date for the police academy, listened to his answer, then wished him well before she said, "Goodnight, Jack."

"Goodnight, Ms. Spencer."

He waved her through and kept the massive hinged panels open until Beck's truck cleared the stone support posts for the huge iron and wood barriers the developer had imported from an ancient Scottish keep. They remained open from six a.m. until eleven p.m. every day. Residents always had the option of entering and leaving from the other private access road via the unmanned sliding gate that was operated by the homeowners' remote controls.

Alexa kept glancing into her rearview mirror even though all she could see was headlights and the general outline of her husband's truck.

She was exhausted and a little worried.

Beck had been quiet since soon after his family's unanimous agreement on their detailed strategy for moving forward. Yes, he had remained engaged with the group as they dug into a simple, hearty dinner of Portia's slow-cooker beef stew with skillet corn bread, and tasty store-bought macaroons and iced hot chocolate for dessert. Through every course, Beck had conversed while also seeming distracted.

Alexa pulled into her three-car garage on the side closest to the door leading into the kitchen, which left the side with extra length for storage space for Beck's truck.

As she got out of her car and walked back to the popped open truck lid to take out her new carryon bag filled with toiletries and clothes she had purchased en route to the airport before boarding the private flight to Las Vegas on Saturday, Alexa hoped she and Beck were not about to have their first serious fight as a couple.

❧❧❧

"Talk to me, Beck."

After taking their luggage to the bedroom that had gone from being her sacred space to being their shared private sanctuary in the past few months, he had joined Alexa in the cozy sitting area next to the kitchen and collapsed into the very frou-frou looking chair that surprised him with its sturdiness every time he sat in it.

He closed his eyes on a groan, not to ignore or dismiss his wife's request for speech, but to give himself a few more seconds to figure out the source of his trouble.

He felt her step between his spread legs. Her subtle scent filled his senses when he inhaled.

"Is this how our first serious fight begins—with your pretending I'm not here, Beck?"

He opened his eyes and shook his head, tilting his chin up to meet her worried gaze. "I'm not pretending you're not here, Lex. I'm relying on your peaceful spirit to calm my restlessness."

He reached up to bracket her waist in his hands and pull her closer until he was able to lean his cheek against her stomach and wrap his arms around her hips. He closed his eyes again.

"I promised my dad I would take care of them. I promised him that I would keep Mom in our home. Make sure the twins grew up strong and independent. That they graduated from high school and college. I was so cavalier about it because my dad was big and strong. He was relatively young—only fifty-three. It was a routine outpatient procedure. That's what I was thinking at the notary's office when I impatiently signed documents that added my name to the deed on the house and made me the twins' temporary guardian the day before I took my dad to the hospital."

One of Alexa's hands cupped his head near the nape of his neck. The other rubbed slow circles across his tense shoulders.

"His heart seized during the procedure. He never regained consciousness. No medical negligence according to the neutral third-party investigative review board, but the hospital paid a settlement and enrolled Mom into one of their ALS treatment studies in exchange for signing documents that we wouldn't pursue litigation at a later date. Dad's life insurance paid off their original mortgage, and his military retirement benefits helped, too.

"Lindsey and Portia were eleven. My mom was already wheelchair bound with severely impeded speech. I had just started my second year as an elementary school art teacher. Relatives were willing to take the girls, but not together."

Alexa felt the weight of his body slump harder against her with his deep sigh.

"I gave up my one-bedroom rental and moved back home. Quality in-home nursing care burned through the hospital settlement in less than three years, but I had developed a modestly profitable side business with illustrating self-published children's books under the name of Sergio Allegra in honor of my parents. My combined income met the requirements to finance a second mortgage."

Alexa curved her body lower and turned her head to angle her ear closer to his mouth when his voice dropped on the last word.

"Some days I dreamed of running away to Paris, France or even Seattle, Washington to escape. I'd immediately feel guilty and disgusted with myself for wanting to punk out," he whispered.

"I scheduled my vasectomy on my thirtieth birthday.

There wasn't much time for dating, but I couldn't risk being responsible for one more person. My mom doesn't know. It would break her heart.

"My original art pieces started selling when the girls were high school freshmen, which gave us some financial breathing room, and allowed me to purchase the warehouse." Beck's voice had resumed its solid pitch.

"I was saving money in the twins' college fund all along even when adding twenty dollars per month was all I could afford. So their academic scholarships for tuition were like hitting the lottery twice on the same day. And the LuxeLinks offer, plus the uptick in the sales of my pieces in the gallery, provided the biggest money cushion my family's ever had—including when my dad was alive.

"Then you and I meet, and it's like here you are, the love I've been dreaming of. But what if my obligations scare you away? Then they don't, and we're exclusive. Then you're being blackmailed, and you think you should break up with me to protect me, which freaks me out because no one has been focused on protecting me since Mom's ALS diagnosis one week after Lindsey and Portia turned two. More than one specialist told us mom wouldn't survive for more than a year.

"Tonight, Lindsey and Portia asserted themselves as capable young adults, and you stepped up, and Lisa did, too. It made me realize that I don't know how to share these responsibilities, Lex. It's all fallen solely on me for nearly a decade."

∽∽

Alexa suspected that Beck didn't know he was crying.

His silent tears soaked the front of her fitted linen dress while his embrace crushed her hips against his chest.

"Beckford Gallegas, you've accomplished all that your father expected of you and more." She cupped his cheekbones between her palms and guided his head back until he looked up into her face. She smiled. "Trust me to share all your burdens. I am your devoted friend, Beck. I am your wife. You are my husband. We are partners. We are confidants. All that I am and all that I have is yours, Beck. Accept the gifts I'm offering to you and offer me the same in return."

His intense dark eyes stared up into hers. The sheen of tears seemed to magnify the potency of his pensive regard until he blinked, then stood, scooping her up into his arms in one uninterrupted flow of movement.

The radiance of his sudden smile glistened between shiny vertical streaks from his tears. "Yes, that's our truth, Lex," he said before she kissed him into closing his eyes and kissing her back with equal enthusiasm. She kept kissing him until his reddened eyes opened halfway and twinkled with mischievous intent as he pivoted to carry her out of the kitchen.

"Let's go to bed."

∽∽

They made it into bed, eventually, after stopping to concentrate on kissing each other into delirious, mutual submission in the two-story atrium that opened into the central gathering space and linked the public areas with the private ones. Moonlight cast down a dreamy glow from the staggered skylights.

Beck's long strides quickly carried them past her home office and guestroom to the oversized door leading to the main suite at the end of the wide hall.

He shouldered through the partially opened door, entering the pitch black sitting area. When Alexa opened her eyes she couldn't see anything—not the sofa, large round storage ottoman or the television mounted on the wall.

Alexa was completely disoriented, but Beck must not have been because he kept kissing her as he continued moving until they crossed the threshold into what had become their bedroom during the past few months.

One wall of privacy glass windows softly illuminated the room with the indirect lighting from the lap pool, but the intensity of Beck's focused gaze into her eyes as he lowered her feet to the bamboo floor narrowed Alexa's focus to his face. With her hands clutching Beck's shoulders, she rocked forward and up onto the tips of her toes, leaning in to resume kissing the stern line of his supple lips framed in a day's worth of dark beard growth.

⁓⁓⁓

Beck clasped his wife's waist and held on while she seduced his mouth with her soft, sweet lips, nips of her sharp teeth, and languid licks of her tongue. He loved being the sole target of her affection while she leaned into him, trusting him to support her weight completely. Her fingers caressed their way from his shoulders to his neck, then to spear into his hair, pulling his head lower.

Alexa's kisses devoured his reason and thoughts beyond any goal other than getting her naked. Beck dragged the skirt of her dress up to her waist before he shoved her skimpy underwear down to her ankles. He palmed her butt to lift her off her feet as he stepped on the silky scrap of fabric around her ankles until it fell off the tips of her high heels.

Beck's tipping forward to drop them onto the bed didn't interrupt their kiss—neither did his one-handed grapple with his belt, button, and zipper. He pushed at his briefs, freed his greedy dick, and shoved hard into the snug, wet clasp of his wife's body. She bit down on his bottom lip with enough pressure to make him jerk as her fingers jerked in his hair and her body arched into his. Body primed, he thrust deeper, pushing a breathless cry from Alexa that broke their kiss, leaving them panting as they stared into each other's eyes.

ↄﻭↄ

Alexa forced herself to hold still. She concentrated

on the differences between the cool textured Matelassé coverlet under her and the warm muscular blanket of Beck's body over her, surrounding her, and his heat within her. The inescapable stretch demanded by the smooth, hot thickness of his erection magnified the abrasive sensation of his heavy belt, metal zipper, and worn denim between her legs and against her inner thighs.

"So good, Lex," he said before making her cry out again by working a little bit deeper. "You always—" He groaned. "—always feel so damn good."

She embraced him with her entire body while they gazed into each other's eyes and breathed in each other's breath until orgasm swelled and filled her senses first, then his.

ecec

An hour later they were both sated, naked, and exhausted as they lay on their stomachs with their heads sharing a pillow. The drawn opaque curtains made the bedroom pitch black.

"The UTG chief of security will want to assign a regular detail to you, Beck," Alexa whispered sleepily.

"Why?" He mildly grumbled his challenge. "I passed his situational awareness, evasive driving, and hand combat training courses."

In the darkness, the weight of his hand stroked over her wild bed head before his callous palm settled gently between her shoulder blades.

"Lex, you can tell Elgin Brown that I said thanks, but no thanks to my own security detail. One for Lindsey and Portia, though, is a different deal." He sounded more than half asleep.

Beck's attitude didn't surprise Alexa, but his mellow tone was the opposite of his reaction months ago during his first meeting with the UTG chief of security. Then, Beck had fumed at the much older man for questioning his ability to keep Alexa and himself safe during their outings as a private couple.

"We'll figure it out, Beck."

"Yes, we will." His soft words sent a puff of minty breath against her face before they both subsided into peaceful slumber.

ᆖᆖ

In her office early the next morning, Alexa tried to tap into last night's peacefulness as her chief of security scolded her.

"You opened a package from an unknown sender, Ms. Spencer. You traveled across the country—twice in a twenty-four-hour timeframe—in non-UTG private jets. With unvetted pilots. With other passengers who were strangers. Without notifying me or your weekend security detail about your travel plans, Ms. Spencer."

Two Ms. Spencers, no matter how calmly spoken, meant that Alexa was on the chief's criminally stupid list.

She knew him well enough to guess that he had waited until Tuesday to talk with her privately in order to let his temper cool.

"Chief Brown." Alexa quietly entreated the former Secret Service agent to sit in the chair next to hers in the conversation area in the corner of her large office suite. "Your summary is mostly accurate. The owner of the fleet of private jets is my sorority sister's brother, who is a retired US Air Force pilot. All of his pilots are honorably discharged or retired military."

"I know, Ms. Spencer."

His tone warmed to a few degrees above his previously arctic levels, and he was no longer glaring his displeasure at her.

"I disclosed everything to the chairman of the board prior to our departure for Las Vegas on Saturday evening, Chief Brown. He signed off on my plan of action."

The corner of Elgin Brown's mouth kicked up in a chagrined impression of a smile. "So he told me on Sunday night when I was planning to ambush you after your press conference."

Alexa slumped back in her chair. "So you're already over your mad, Chief Brown?"

He nodded. "Yes, Ms. Spencer." He chuckled in response to her exaggerated frown. "I am completely recovered from my upset over what initially appeared to be your cavalier attitude toward your personal and professional safety.

"Two things, if something similar happens again, Ms. Spencer: One, call your security detail to handle the package in a less populated area. Two, allow your security detail to plug any unauthorized tech into the isolated units we keep on hand solely for that purpose. Smart move with using a new prepaid cell to contact the chairman on his encrypted satellite phone."

He leaned toward Alexa with a gleeful smile on his craggy face. "Now, let's talk security arrangements for your new family members."

CHAPTER 7

Beck looked up at the sound of knuckles rapping against the seasoned wood of his open classroom door.

"Reverend Matt," he said, pausing in the act of sorting graded assignments and restocking the art supplies his five classes had depleted. He reached out to shake his new father-in-law's hand.

The much older man used the connection to reel in Beck for a brief, back-slapping hug. "Please call me dad if that's comfortable for you, Beckford," he said as he set a wicker picnic basket on the enormous drafting table that Beck used as his desk. "Roast beef sandwiches on organic homemade rye with grilled heirloom tomatoes." He settled atop the metal stool next to the desk. "Close the door, please, son, we've got family business to discuss."

An hour later, Beck sat in speechless awe.

The generosity of Rev. Matthew Spencer's candor about his life with Alexa's mother revealed insightful details. While savoring their sandwiches and chilled bottles of locally brewed non-alcoholic cider, Beck listened to his father-in-law's adventures as a poor itinerant pastor who found the love of his life when he stopped to help a beautiful young woman change her flat tire.

"Her Volkswagon Bug was a nauseating shade of putrid green, but it ran like factory new once she started it again. It purred smoother than my slightly newer sedan ever had.

"When I refused to accept payment, Luccia Davis pulled a flyer from her back pocket and invited me to a reception at a nearby community rec center. She said I could follow her if I wanted to.

"I looked at that voluptuous, gorgeous brown young woman with a dark reddish brown afro framing her lovely face, tie-dyed T-shirt and tight, faded, hip-hugging bell bottom jeans wrapped around her body, and I said yes. She intrigued me—and the flyer mentioned free food.

"Turns out that she was being honored by her neighbors for winning an international architectural design competition for college undergrads."

Beck heard the older man's pride and love in his wife and her accomplishments. Beck recognized the other man's gratitude as Rev. Matt talked about their correspondence courtship.

"Luccia received offers from multiple prestigious firms her senior year, but she chose a quirky little firm in upstate New York because they were specializing in environmentally sustainable design and construction practices for municipal buildings.

"I got an assistant minister post at Blessed Redeemer, a progressive church near Rhinebeck. The salary was a pittance, but one of the few benefits was free housing in a cozy two-bedroom cottage on the church's property.

"We married the week after Luccia's college graduation."

Beck asked, "How did you end up in White Plains from Rhinebeck?" The question sent Rev. Matt off on another tangent.

"Luccia was pregnant with our first child, who turned out to be Alexa, and my wife wanted to move on to a bigger firm after her maternity leave ended. Again, multiple prestigious firms courted her. This time she chose a very large firm with diverse interests in rehab and new construction of residential and commercial structures.

"Holy Savior Church in Bronxville hired me to be their interim pastor when theirs died in a car accident. Employment benefits included a two-bedroom house that was twice the square footage as our first home."

Beck chewed the last bite of his sandwich as Reverend Matt talked about being the primary caregiver to Alexa, then Marie, Davida, and finally, Matt, Jr. while his interim position turned permanent and his congregation grew exponentially.

"It was providing access to affordable childcare from state-certified caregivers through our collaboration with a licensed training program that made us a wealthy church. Those revenues financed our runaway outreach ministry, mental health, and substance abuse recovery programs.

"Someone we helped in those early years donated the land where we built the current church two decades ago. Luccia donated her professional skills to design and project manage, and she tithes the gross of her income to the church every week even though we've made a habit of visiting a new church every Sunday now that M.J. is the senior pastor.

"My wife earns more in a year than I have earned in my entire life, Beckford. Before I went back to school after Matt, Jr. graduated high school, my only academic credential was an Associate's Degree in pastoral counseling. And for some people, those facts make me less of a man…"

Beck looked into his father-in-law's steady gaze and smiled in gratitude for the unsolicited wise counsel he hadn't realized he needed. He kept listening while Reverend Matt kept sharing.

"…it helps if you decide in advance how or if you're going to respond when someone mistakenly calls you Mr. Spencer or does it to needle you, Beckford. Luccia and I have been married for fifty-one years. Everyone who

knows us well knows that she goes by Davis professionally and Spencer privately, but it's still not unusual for
someone to call me Reverend Davis when we're together.

"So think about how you'll respond, and talk to my
daughter when it pricks your pride. Don't let it fester and
grow beyond petty annoyance. Consider your life without
Alexa in it, then ask yourself if that's your desired outcome. I'm glad you're a strong, self-confident man,
Beckford, because that's the very least of what it takes to
be married to a powerful woman, to ignore the snide,
outdated remarks about who's the alpha in your relationship. Who's the boss? Who wears the pants? Society has
changed since Luccia and I married. The world has
changed. You and Alexa are so much younger. My prayer
is that you won't experience the same harsh judgment
and stinging verbal barbs we have."

Beck watched Reverend Matt gather up their empty
bottles, sandwich wrappers, and fabric napkins and place
them in the picnic basket before he stood.

Beck stood then stepped forward to initiate a farewell embrace. "Thank you." Beck pulled back to look
into his father-in-law's smiling gaze. "Thank you, Dad."

The older man's smile broadened into a pleased
chuckle. He pounded Beck's shoulder. "My pleasure,
son."

ↄ⊰ↄ

UTG Security Chief Elgin Brown was leaning

against a black SUV parked between Beck's truck and Rev. Matt's chauffeured sedan.

Chief Brown said, "Good talking to you, John," to the driver before he nodded at Rev. Matt and Beck.

"Reverend Spencer," he said, stringing out the three syllables of the honorific in a scolding tone of voice.

"Chief Brown, permitting John to drive me here was a compromise. Driving myself was my preference." He tilted his head toward the driver, who took the picnic basket from his hand. "John's promise to wait outside is the only reason he's with me."

Chief Brown closed his eyes. Beck was pretty sure the security chief was reciting the rosary before he inhaled deeply and opened his eyes.

"Reverend Spencer, your wife and your daughter are wealthy, powerful women. Blood-thirsty religious zealots have labeled you a heretic for your progressive, inclusive approach to spreading the Christian gospel, even though you've stepped aside into the position of pastor emeritus in favor of your son," Chief Brown said. "Your wife and daughter would never forgive themselves or me if someone harmed you."

Reverend Matt glanced sideways at Beck.

"Chief Brown plays the guilt card with great effectiveness," he whispered loudly enough for all of the men to hear as he got into the backseat of his sedan.

Reverend Matt powered down the tinted window and saluted Chief Brown after John closed the car door.

"Protecting that cagey preacher man is penance for the sins of my misspent youth," Chief Brown said conversationally as he and Beck watched the chauffeured sedan leave the nearly empty school parking lot.

"Beckford," he said, turning to face him.

Beck laughed. "Pitch your voice an octave higher and squint your eyes while you jut your chin at me, Chief Brown, and you'll have exactly duplicated my sister Lindsey's expression of long-suffering annoyed impatience with me."

The security chief was fighting a smile as he shook his head. In the next instant, his humor vanished. "Ms. Spencer says it's your choice about your security detail."

Beck simply looked at the other man and waited.

Chief Brown sighed. "If you agree to armoring the undercarriage and passenger compartment of your truck and bullet-proof glass, I'll sign off on no security shadow for you when you're solo."

Beck was pleased, but he had come to understand some basic truths about Chief Brown's dedication to his mission. "But…"

"But one of my seasoned agents has a degree in art therapy. Your principal is willing to accept him as a full-time volunteer teacher's aide for your classes."

Which told Beck that Chief Brown had been working this angle for weeks if his agent had already cleared all of the public school system's numerous background checks and administrative hurdles.

"His presence will add a layer of protection for all of the students and staff, not just you, Beckford."

Beck nodded his acknowledgement of being outmaneuvered.

"Reverend Matt was correct, Chief Brown, you're very effective."

"We have a deal?"

"Yes."

"Good, because your mom signed off on the home security upgrades and your sisters start situational awareness training, evasive driving techniques, and hand combat boot camp this weekend."

∽∽∽

Seeing Beck's truck appear in the widening gap of the upwardly scrolling garage door made Alexa smile as she pulled into the slot closest to the door leading into the kitchen. So did seeing his boots and running shoes neatly aligned on the Sisal mat immediately inside the doorway. Alexa kicked out of her heels.

A deep breath filled her head with the scents of freshly baked bread, roasted vegetables, and grilled meat.

Although she had come home to find Beck waiting for her with nourishing food and his undivided attention many nights during the past few months, knowing that he was now here as a permanent resident and her lawfully wedded husband deepened her joy in ways she hadn't expected.

"Beck?" she called softly, making her way across the cool interior to the warming oven on the far wall. The interior light showed a covered ceramic dish on the top rack.

Her mouth watered, but she pivoted away from her dinner and kept moving through their home until she found Beck laid out on the bamboo flooring in the dimly lit atrium. His eyes were closed. His body relaxed into corpse pose with his phone almost touching his blunt fingertips. The slow rise and fall of his chest and the absence of blood or any other signs of injury smothered her initial surge of alarm.

"Thank you for making dinner and saving some for me, Beck. Should I ask you why you're lying on the cold, hard floor when you're only steps away from several pieces of very comfortable furniture?" she asked as she knelt at his side, then stretched along the length of his strong body when he opened his arms to her without opening his eyes.

It took them only a few moments of flirty jostling to get settled with Alexa's head tucked under his bristly chin, with Beck's arm around her shoulders, and her arm draped across the threadbare cotton of his T-shirt covering his taut stomach.

"The owner of the gallery wants me to do a private exhibition of all the pieces in my 'Defiant' series."

Alexa waited. His pause lasted long enough for the pace of their breathing to synchronize into a steady rise and fall of her breasts against his chest.

"She wants to host a black-tie, invitation only shin-dig next month because her voice mailbox is full, the gallery phone has been ringing non-stop since she opened Monday morning, her site crashed yesterday afternoon, and her foot traffic has increased exponentially," he whispered in the gruff voice of a man who was mystified by the sudden achievement of his heart's most treasured desire.

Alexa stroked a vague figure-eight pattern down one side of his obliques to his thigh, then back up to his hip to his side in continuous loops.

"My pieces are formed from discarded materials, Lex. Who's going to dress up to come see my reconfig-ured trash?"

Alexa rolled and scooted until she lay atop Beck as an only slightly softer, much warmer perch than the floor. She used a two-handed grip on his shoulders to slide her body up to face him nose to nose. "All of your art pieces are refined, Beckford Gallegas. Your technique with in-tegrating natural materials with manmade components and transforming them into organic shapes compels the eyes, expands the mind, and touches the spirit."

She wiggled her mons against his erection as she kissed his lips. "Plus, your art is fun and interesting, and your beautiful furniture is also a gorgeous balance of masculine and feminine elements. Do you need the table for the exhibit"?

The round banquet table in the formal dining room had only been in place for a month, but since the first moment of its installation Alexa had felt as if the thin layers of wood, stone, and glass set upon a base of several latticed chairbacks trussed together with thin bands of hammered copper belonged in the sunny space just like the man belonged in her life, and her heart, as if he had been created for her.

"No," he said. "I told her that our personal furniture and decorative pieces are off-limits. She didn't argue, which tells me she wants to keep me happy so I won't seriously consider any of these new offers for representing me."

Lying atop the muscular mat of her husband's body, Alexa looked into his serious face and listened to him describe the hundreds of emails filling his school address inbox. "...there are some propositions, money pleas, and requests for help from Nigerian princes, but most of them are from legitimate art dealers, gallery owners, furniture companies, talent management teams—even an art book publisher, Lex—" His deep sigh lifted, then lowered her like she was riding a breaking wave at the shoreline. "—if the personal assistant for the snooty artist rep who called my ethos primitive eco-dreck, after flipping through my portfolio last year, hadn't just called me an hour ago to invite me to lunch this weekend, I'd, I'd..."

His bewildered voice trailed away to nothing. "Ouch," he grumped when Alexa pinched him.

His palms squeezed her butt in retaliation before she said, "You are not dreaming, Beck. Our situation brought your art to their attention, but your dedicated study, your hard work, and talent will keep you in the spotlight because you've earned these opportunities." Alexa wanted to keep hammering away at the self-questioning vulnerability she saw in his dark eyes, but she forced herself to remain silent for as long as it took for him to confess his deepest fear aloud to her, and to himself.

ↄ౩ↄ

Beck felt his wife's willingness to lie atop him and look down into his face all night if that was how long it took for him to speak the bitter truth.

"None of them would be interested in me or my work if I weren't married to you, Lex. If the announcement of our marriage hadn't generated media buzz with the potential for sexual scandal and corporate mayhem, that elitist prick of an artist rep wouldn't have invited me to lunch."

Lex nodded. "That's true of the newcomers, Beck. Most people are followers, and the math of supply and demand requires it. But that's not true of the owner of the gallery who's been selling your art on consignment for the past three years and wants to host an exclusive one-man exhibit next month. It's not true of the collectors who bought your work before Sunday. It's not true of the self-published authors who hired you to illustrate their award-winning children's books. The municipalities that hired you to paint murals and execute statuary for their public spaces have recognized your talents for years."

Hearing the pride in her voice made him smile and think of the complete set of every book he had illustrated sitting on their own designated shelf in Lex's home office and a montage of professionally framed photos of his murals and statues on the walls.

"Plenty of discerning people recognized the value in your artistry, Beck, and invested in you before we ever met. And I hope you told that snooty rep's personal assistant that you will never be available to either of them for anything ever again. There's a pop song about it. Send the audio file to them."

Beck laughed before he kissed the fierce pout of her lush lips. When needing to breathe forced them to pause, he said, "I politely declined the lunch invitation and made it clear that any future overtures would receive the same response."

Lex sat up, straddling his waist and clapping as she smiled down at him. "Oh, good, now we celebrate," she said, sliding backward and dragging the wet heat between her legs over his crotch until she settled into place on his thighs and eased the elastic waistband of his workout shorts and briefs over his hard dick.

"Which lips first, Beck?"

"Lady's choice, Lex."

He silently thanked every deity he'd ever heard of as she slowly lowered her head and opened her mouth, bathing his crotch in her warm breath.

At midnight, they sat at the kitchen table and shared Lex's dried out dinner while she wore only his confiscated t-shirt and he wore only his workout shorts. He now owed her another pair of fancy underwear.

CHAPTER 8

Beck halfway woke up a minute before the alarm sounded, filling the bedroom with the swelling refrain of music that sounded like Ravel to his cottony ears. Pale illumination nudged his closed eyelids, so Lex had raised the blackout drapes. Reaching out and touching Lex's side of the bed confirmed what his other senses and vague pre-dawn impressions of being thoroughly kissed, then hearing, "Love you, Beck. See you Friday night," before feeling Lex slip out of his arms and out of bed.

When he opened his eyes and turned his head, Beck saw dark swirls of writing on the optic white rectangle and remembered something about an undercover surprise inspection of a solar-powered UTG manufacturing facility in North Dakota.

Beck rolled out of bed and stretched as he walked into his designated closet space to grab swim trunks off of a shelf and thought about using their three days of separation to check in with his mom and sisters after school then stay at his studio to finish more pieces for his upcoming show. None of that would really distract him from missing Lex, but he hopped that keeping busy would make the next three days pass quickly.

Laps in the pool at maximum speed for ten minutes were a good way to jumpstart his day and the countdown to his reunion with his wife.

෯෯෯

Mid-flight from Westchester, New York to Minot, North Dakota in her window seat in coach, Alexa heard her phone vibrate in the rhythm she'd chosen to notify her of activity in her pool. The phone pulsed in her handbag on the empty seat next to her. Seconds later, she was watching a dot move up and down the length of the pool in her backyard.

If the human body represented by the dot stopped moving and sank to the bottom and stayed there for more than ten seconds, the sensors would trigger a nine-one-one call from her home security system.

She and Beck usually deactivated the safety feature when they swam together. Recalling some of their adult water play made Alexa smile as she watched the dot and imagined her husband's fit body slicing through the calm turquoise water in plain black swim trunks that framed the flow of his strong torso into his muscular glutes and legs. Beck was beautiful inside and out.

When the dot stopped moving eleven minutes later, and *empty pool* flashed across her screen, Alexa texted Beck: *Now we're both wet.*

She was listening to her shuttle driver's recommendations for local restaurants to visit by the time she read his reply: You're a cruel tease, woman.

She smiled but didn't continue the exchange because she was moments away from the beginning of her performance as a mid-level operations evaluator for UTG USA. Production was mysteriously down at the Minot, North Dakota plant and Alexa needed to walk the lines and talk to the workers in order to course correct. She would privately make her arrival known to the site manager and head engineer as a professional courtesy, and because both women had met with Alexa several times over the years. They were likely to recognize her.

She'd never used the name of Dominique Foster before, but her disguise of dated makeup, straightened, slicked back hair, and frumpy clothes probably wouldn't hold up to intense scrutiny from the two women.

ⅇⲟⲉⲟ

By lunch break for the second shift, Alexa had a

good idea about the source of the productivity slow down, and it wasn't because of the grainy black and white images of Beck from Sunday night's press conference. Stud, hottie, Latin heartthrob, and other true and objectifying terms were handwritten across the array of copier paper pages covering one wall in the women's locker room, but even her husband's considerable appeal wasn't enough to reverse the tide of low morale that swamped the facility.

Beck would hate this display as much as he hated the viral memes of their image superimposed onto the original and remake King Kong movie posters, the Lebron James and Giselle photo, and assorted iconic images of a more delicate woman who's being held in the implacable grip of an aggressive male figure.

Now, Alexa was scrolling through the computer documentation for the last two years of promotions, performance commendations, warnings, demotions, terminations, and voluntary separations. She went back to the hotel and sorted her thoughts on all she'd observed and read.

❧❦❧

"Lex." Her husband sounded wide awake at midnight on the east coast.

"Beck, why aren't you sleeping? I was trying to leave you a good-morning voice message."

Soft metal clangs and shuffles answered her question

before he said, "Came to the warehouse after dinner at Mom's. Just finished a smaller piece and getting ready to sketch out a design for a new idea then go to bed and dream of you."

Water sloshed when Alexa shifted in her cooling bath with deflating bubbles.

"You're in the tub, Lex."

The drop in the pitch and volume of his voice started a shiver in her ear. The husky sound radiated sexual interest and sensual speculation that filled her senses and primed her body with longing for more than his words.

Alexa raised one leg to rest along the edge of the tub.

"What are you doing, Lex?"

She sighed.

"Spreading my legs and wishing you were here with me now, Beck. Feeling the water caress my skin, slide between my labia and inside my vagina, over my stomach and around my breasts. Being surrounded and inundated and embraced by the water makes me long for your breath, your hands, your body, your dick."

❦

His wife's breathy confessions floated to him to the accompaniment of sounds of splashing water against skin and porcelain.

"Making me jack off in the shower this morning after reading your 'Now we're both wet' text when I got out of the pool wasn't enough torture, Lex? You want me hard and awake all night, imagining you naked and wet."

One-handed, Beck unbuttoned and unzipped his heavy canvas work pants and reached into his briefs to grab his dick. He squeezed, groaning at the immense pleasure of the brutal pressure that didn't really relieve the ultimate ache of missing Lex.

"Here's your payback," he said, then groaned and panted as he worked his flesh until he came fast and hard with a loud, growling cry.

∽∽∽

Eyes closed, Alexa jerked her head away from her phone while the primitive cry of her husband's release rang in her ears and echoed throughout her body from clitoris to womb to nipples to the clenched muscles of her anus, but she didn't touch herself. She clutched her phone in one hand while the splayed fingers of her other hand gripped the rounded edge of the deep bathtub. She pulled her phone closer to her ear again and heard Beck's heavy breathing.

"I'm imagining that the water flowing between my legs is your breath, your touch, your semen, Beck. Coming into me; seeping out of me." Her breath hitched. Her inner thighs trembled with the tightening of her muscles from her vagina outward until she vibrated with the tremors of impending orgasm from her parted lips to her flexed toes. The sudden impact of coming bowed her back and arched her neck as she choked out a scream.

Long moments later, Alexa heard Beck's voice say, "No more sexual gratification for either of us, Lex, until we're together again. Deal?"

"Deal. Goodnight. Love you, Beck."

"Love you just as much, Lex, maybe more. Goodnight."

CHAPTER 9

Very early Thursday morning Alexa, still in disguise for the benefit of everyone other than the nine people in this small meeting room with her, asked, "Why are you rewarding your favorites and penalizing everyone else?" Alexa looked directly into the eyes of each person who was seated at the conference table in the isolated room. "Everyone who answers honestly has an opportunity to save their careers at UTG."

It took four hours and one meal ordered in to dislodge the whole truth of the matter. By the time they departed at eight p.m., they had outlined a strategy of redress, corrections, and meritocracy over personal favoritism with performance benchmarks and timelines as concrete measures of improvement.

Friday morning, Alexa addressed the day shift as

herself to acknowledge the plant's vulnerabilities and to share an overview of their strategy for building a stronger team in which each member's contributions were recognized and rewarded.

All of the other work shifts would gather in the auditorium to see the recorded video throughout the day.

Exhausted, Alexa nearly cried with joy when she saw Beck standing on the unrestricted side of the security queue. His ball cap, sunglasses, and loose sweats didn't fool her eye. He was holding a small white poster board sign with *BELOVED* printed in the best version of his messy scrawl.

Both grinning, he dropped his sign, and she dropped the telescoping luggage handle on her carryon bag and fell into each other's arms.

"What are you doing here, Beck?" she asked as they squeezed each other breathless and gently swayed. "One of Chief Brown's drivers was supposed to take me to meet you at the warehouse."

She felt his chin nudge the top of her mostly still straightened hair.

"Yeah, she's circling the departures drop-off loop. You sounded totally done when we talked earlier, so I got Chief Brown to okay my plan to hijack your ride, and I changed our destination to home for the weekend. We can wallow undisturbed until Sunday morning."

He nuzzled his scruffy cheek against hers.

Alexa looked up into the double reflection of her

weary self in his aviator shades perched on his conquistador's nose above the half smile on his kissable lips.

"But you need to finish some artworks-in-progress this weekend."

Beck's half smile spread to include every muscle in his face. "Add missing you to sexual frustration and I got two pieces completed after working through half the night Wednesday and yesterday, Lex."

He stooped to pick up his sign and grabbed the extended luggage handle in one hand on his way back up to his full height while he laced the fingers of his other hand with hers, tugging as he stepped toward the exit doors.

"Time to make out in the backseat," he said.

"Like teenagers going to prom?" she asked.

"Like newlyweds who've been reunited after being separated for three very long days, Lex."

⁗⁘⁗

The notification chime drew Margeaux's gaze from the land conservancy documents spread across her desk to her phone on the corner of the large surface. She laughed aloud when she brought up the unauthorized fan page for Beckford Gallegas.

After skimming over a string of emojis, cryptic abbreviations, acronyms, hashtags, Gifs and exclamation marks, she swiped through the photo timeline that started with images from Sunday night's press conference, continued with blurry shots of him as he entered his family's home, and ended with pictures of a man holding a sign with BELOVED handwritten on it. The geo location and time stamp labeled Westchester Airport as the place and fifteen minutes earlier as the time.

Most of the comments praised Beck's looks, his attitude and speculated about his sexual appetite, kinks, stamina, body grooming habits, and penis size without any mention of his new wife except for a few references to Alexa as one lucky old black hag or bitch or feminist or destroyer of traditional family values or harbinger of End Times.

Margeaux tapped the play icon for the recently posted video and choked up a little as she watched the Beckford-shaped man shrouded in ubiquitous athletic wear embrace the beautiful woman who was clearly Alexa even with the significantly less voluminous hair style, casual clothes, and flat shoes.

Margeaux sighed and slouched back in her padded desk chair when the video ended as Beckford and Alexa held hands and stepped out into the night.

Their love story felt like her reward for a job well done. Every successful match, whether temporary or permanent, eased a little bit of her lingering heartache over her mother's suicide.

Decades ago, wealthy, naïve heiress Camilla Marie Carr hadn't had anyone to warn her away from sophisticated predators like Margeaux's father, John Snelling

Hirsch, or to teach her how to recognize con artists and their games, but Margeaux and her sisters would continue to do both through their LuxeLinks Club.

CHAPTER 10
EPILOGUE

One month later:

An hour and a half before their influential guests were scheduled to arrive, Beck watched Lex read his handwritten notecard, which was framed on an easel next to the first sculpture in his "Defiant" series.

Defiant No. 1
I met a woman today.

The metal figure was definitely feminine and dynamic, sensuous and strong in its undulating hammered panels, which seemed to move forward and back according to the observer's line of sight.

"Oh, Beck," she whispered, reaching back to grab his hand and draw him closer as she circled the first sculpture twice clockwise and once counter-clockwise before moving toward number two.

Defiant No. 2
Her direct gaze invites me to see her.
To be seen by her challenges me.

Alexa had seen these two and pieces three and four only in photos and video because they'd sold before she and Beck had made the transition from platonic business companions to exclusive lovers. She'd learned about Beck's notes as captions and chronology last night just before they drifted to sleep after making love, but she hadn't translated his whispered, "My notes are titles to each chapter of our story, Lex, and frame each piece to mean, 'Here's the revelation of my heart and soul.'"

Defiant No. 3
She is a mysterious mirror.

Defiant No. 4
Her surface reflects her clues—and reveals mine, too.

Seeing works five through eleven in the gallery setting made studying them a new experience for Alexa even though she had seen them in various stages of development from pencil sketches to disassembled components during her visits to Beck's warehouse studio. Now, more than half of them had placards with "on loan through the generosity of..." to acknowledge the prescient collectors who were savvy enough to use the exhibit to gloat in a sophisticated manner about their eye for talent and their trendsetting tastes, which also increased the valuation of their entire collections.

Defiant No. 11
She defies all of my limitations.

Her love for him filled her up. Turning and hugging him was all she could do at that moment to express her overwhelming pride and gratitude and joy for every step that had brought their lives together.

❧❧❧

Beck wasn't sure if it was emotion or his wife's tight hug that was making it so hard for him to take a full breath, but the why of it didn't matter. As he and Alexa embraced amid Chief Brown's security team, the gallery's new security team, bustling catering staff and the hovering gallery owner, Beck savored being held by the love of his life.

CHAPTER 11

This Mark Evens the Odds
The LuxeLinks Club Story 2

Twenty Years Ago:

The day after Jaime Lowenthal accepted three dollars in quarters, nickels, and dimes from Miss Margeaux Hirsch in exchange for representing the eight-year-old and her two younger sisters', Julianna and Chloe's, best interests regarding the handling of their trust funds from their recently deceased mother, he recognized an older, harder, masculine version of Margeaux in the man now seated in front of his desk.

John Snelling Hirsch's toasted brown curls were tame compared to his oldest daughter's adorably wild mop. Disappointment and cynicism added menace to his dark gaze, which Margeaux's innocent one lacked. His medium complexion was burnished into a tough hide on the opposite end of the softness scale from the look of her delicate round features. The Hirsch sisters' father radiated power, privilege, strength, and confidence. It was easy for Jaime to believe that their emotionally fragile mother had killed herself in the aftermath of losing him to embezzlement and romantic betrayal.

"How much will it cost me to get you to drop my daughters from your client list, Mr. Lowenthal?"

Jaime's outrage instantly engaged his mouth.

"Please leave right now, Mr. Hirsch." He surprised himself with how calm and courteous his voice sounded when inside he was seething with resentment, on behalf of his newest, youngest clients.

❧❦☙

John Snelling Hirsch admired the young attorney's quick reply and professional delivery despite the look in his eyes. If looks and thoughts could kill, John would have been executed on the spot by the daggers shooting from Jaime Lowenthal's murderous glare. Good. That's the only kind of person John trusted to protect his daughters' best interests.

"You'll do, Mr. Lowenthal. You'll do."

❧❦☙

It took Jaime a second to realize that he had passed some kind of test, which did very little to lessen his anger until the other man leaned forward and said, "Last night, Margeaux initiated hugging me for the first time since Camilla's death."

Speculative thoughts totally thrown out of order, Jaime asked, "How is that related to me?"

After a small sigh, his clients' father said, "Margeaux is a worrier. She's old enough to understand what happened between her mother and me in ways that Jules and Chloe can't. Mrs. Brown is the one who found you and convinced me to allow Margeaux to hire you. Mrs. Brown told me that having a trustworthy advocate would make my daughter feel safe and maybe eventually stop the chronic headaches, upset stomachs, and sleep walking she's suffered since Camilla and I split."

❧❧

Last night at the New Amsterdam library branch, Jaime had researched the whirlwind courtship, fairytale wedding, extended European honeymoon, and first six years of the marriage of gem mining heiress Camilla Marie Carr to John Snelling Hirsch of the New England department stores Hirsches.

Archived newspaper articles from the society pages documented the evolution and disintegration of their union from romantic start to emotionally catastrophic end through continuous slides of the microfiche reader.

Jaime also knew that Mr. Hirsch was now married to the gold-digging tramp Margeaux had mentioned yesterday. They were expecting their first child together within the month.

"Well, most third graders might find it stressful to grieve the loss of their mother while living with the people who contributed to the circumstances of that loss, Mr. Hirsch. Are the girls seeing a therapist?" Keeping his tone civil was still a challenge.

"Margeaux and Jules, but not the baby. Chloe just started speaking recognizable English. She calls Franca her mama."

So in addition to dealing with her mother's suicide, living with her adulterous father and the woman with whom he had cheated who was now his pregnant wife and her stepmother, Margeaux had to listen to her baby sister call that woman Mama.

Because Jaime thought he glimpsed discomfort generated by a smidgen of shame in the other man's eyes, he asked, "Was the money and the sex worth it, Mr. Hirsch?"

৵৩৻৹

John knew from Mrs. Brown that he was ten years older than Jaime Lowenthal, but at that moment he felt like an irresponsible younger man who was being held accountable by a disappointed elder.

"My actions drove the only woman who's ever loved me just for me to commit suicide. Margeaux loves me, but she doesn't trust me. Jules swings back and forth. Chloe will probably hate me and Franca when she's old enough to understand."

His sudden smile felt monstrous on his face and must have looked hideous, based on the young attorney's sudden backward jerk.

"But the remaining Hirsch department stores are thriving again, and the Hirsch family finances are solvent again after a generation of decline."

John had come to the office with the intention of revealing himself and his motives to Jaime Lowenthal if the attorney proved to be a worthy advocate for his daughters, but he couldn't force himself to make the most damning confession: On the day she killed herself, Camilla sent him a note on her monogrammed linen stock with *I would have helped you, John, if you had asked me. Cami* carefully written with her distinctive cursive flair.

Instead, John looked directly into the judgmental gaze of the man who had made his daughter feel less afraid. "Every successful con artist knows that the mark's deepest desire is the most irresistible bait. I'm going to teach you how to spot a con, Mr. Lowenthal, and you're going to teach my daughters."

CHAPTER 12

Present Day:

The team of three Department of Justice investigators temporarily assigned to the New York branch of the Interstate Vice Squad's prostitution task force took notes as they watched the video of Margeaux Hirsch's Bait and Snitch: Spot Five Key Lures of an Effective Con being projected onto the wall of the conference room.

"People dish out how much to hear Miss Moneybags school them on how to avoid getting swindled?" one of the five IVS task force lead agents asked.

"Zip for the video. It's available online. It's the best-selling *Don't Get Duped: Save Yourself and Your Money* series of books and seminars that cost money."

The task force leader's sharp gaze swept the gathering of eight seasoned public servants under her command. "Margeaux Hirsch has dedicated her life to teaching people how to recognize a con game. Her mother's tragic story lends her credibility, but I guess an influential someone does not appreciate Miss Hirsch's success because there's a whisper campaign against her. Anonymous tipsters suggesting that her new LuxeLinks Beach Club is really going to be an exclusive whorehouse for very wealthy, powerful women."

Jonathan James Tiptree sat in the back of the room and heard the message between his boss's words: The whispers had reached the attorney general's ears. Someone was privately challenging her to defend her public assertions that absolutely no one was above the law. During the current AG's tenure, more sex traffickers, their networks, and their affiliated legitimate businesses had been dismantled than at any other time in modern US history.

"LuxeLinks recruits through recommendations from employers who notice when their employees are strapped for cash: frequent requests for over-time, reducing their 401k contributions, borrowing from their retirement funds, taking on a second or third job, and similar behaviors."

After hearing that laundry list of indicators, Jon wasn't surprised when his boss's gaze swung his way.

"Jon, you're going in as a candidate to become an

on-call platonic companion. I've already submitted your name along with the required three letters of recommendation from your professional associates." She named herself, his agency mentor, and the director. "After we get a current headshot of you, we'll messenger the completed application over to her. Ms. Hirsch signed off on accepting the results from last month's agency physical to meet the requirement for medical clearance. Yes, Jon, we want Margeaux Hirsch to know that big guns are aimed at her. She'll take you on either to prove that her exclusive club is not a front for a felonious pandering operation or to show you she's deactivated that part of her business. Either way, the AG saves face without being forced to prosecute one of the governor's most ardent supporters.

"The governor's opponents would love another Eliot Spitzer moment. Have the contact details for your three personal references with you when you go to the initial interview. Expect to receive an old-fashioned paper invitation to lunch at NoSqua House, where Ms. Hirsch will evaluate your table manners in addition to your answers to her questions."

"What if she rejects me?"

One of his happily married female colleagues laughed before she said, "You're so fine, Tree, that Miss Moneybags may decide to keep you as her very own personal arm candy."

Jon laughed along with everyone else on the team because she was right. This wasn't the first time his boss had exploited the genetic jackpot of his looks as a honey stick to infiltrate a hetero female suspect's domain. Saving his parents' home from foreclosure and subsidizing his divorced younger sister's nursing aide income to support her and her four young children meant that he was always looking for legal ways to earn more money, which was common knowledge among his coworkers. His real life offered the perfect cover for this investigation.

ℰ⃨ℰ⃨

Margeaux watched Jonathan James Tiptree move with the unself-conscious grace of a confident man on a mission among the cozy groupings of custom-crafted furniture. He kept his eyes on the table she was sharing with Uncle J. Low on the upper terrace of the private social club called NoSqua House with its views of the northern square of 10th Avenue and the High Line.

"He's very intense," her family by choice said under his breath as they watched the federal agent's approach.

The tailored sports coat, crisp white dress shirt, and dark jeans adhered to the dress code. The scuffed black cowboy boots toed the line of appropriateness, but the NoSqua House gatekeeper had been a very popular LuxeLinks companion with their QUILTBAG members before Margeaux recommended Nicole for her current post, which was in a different universe from her previous job as a bouncer at a QUILTBAG meat market dive across town. As a result, Nicole allowed LuxeLinks candidates more leeway with the dress code than she would grant to other non-member guests.

Intense had been Margeaux's reaction after her first look at Jonathan James Tiptree's eight by ten headshot enclosed in the completed application his boss had messengered to Margeaux as requested. Dark hair, well-proportioned ears, and a strong jaw perfectly framed the stern line of his unsmiling lips, sharp cheekbones, and prominent nose beneath the piercing directness of his dark eyes. Long dark eyelashes were the only delicate features etched across the taut canvas of his weathered skin. The look in his eyes clearly projected his stoic impatience.

Jonathan looked hard and hardened. He looked strong. Appealing enough to inspire Margeaux to an extended session of pleasuring herself. She'd begun by lying naked in the center of her queen-sized bed, which she'd stripped down to its fitted sheet. Spreading her legs made it easy for her to place both of her hands around her vulva and stroke and squeeze her labia while her clitoris swelled and stiffened. Stretching her hands between her legs straightened her arms, which pushed her breasts together into a double-tipped mound between her flexed triceps.

Seeing her stiff nipples and feeling the tingle of her escalating arousal made her briefly regret that she wasn't flexible enough to suckle her own breasts as she worked two fingers of one hand into the clutch of her sopping wet vagina.

She closed her eyes, picturing Jonathan James Tiptree, imagining his fingers pumping hard and fast in the snug channel of her sex—not her own fingers.

Margeaux thumped the heel of her other hand against her mons hard enough to make herself cry out at the jolt. She did again. And again, before lightly stroking her slippery clitoris until the almost painful stimulation drew continuous moans, from her gulping throat, as she drew her knees up with her feet flat against the mattress.

She pumped her hips up to meet each downstroke. More wetness pooled around her plunging fingers to trickle between her buttocks and gather at her clenched anal bud.

Her loud cries muted the sounds of wet friction as she pushed harder to penetrate deeper. Pressing the heel of her hand even harder against her mons pinched her clitoris against her fingertip, rocketing her primed body into orgasm. Her vaginal muscles clamped down on her fingers as her hips lifted and her back arched until only her head and, shoulders, and feet touched the bed while she thrashed and screamed through the conflagration.

Seconds later, Margeaux collapsed into a wrung-out heap of sweaty, satisfied flesh and rattled bones.

That was how intensely she had responded to a picture of his face days ago and every night since. Now, with the source of her heated fantasies almost within touching proximity, she wondered how meeting the man would impact her reaction to him.

To Uncle J. Low, she said, "Intensity works in a LuxeLinks companion as long as it's backed with intelligence and honor. Let's see if Agent Tiptree embodies the trifecta."

CHAPTER 13

Jon's first look at Margeaux Carr Hirsch in the natural light of the midday sun on the sparsely populated upper terrace of the casually sophisticated private club revealed what professional headshots, descriptions in gossip blogs, and images from paparazzi ambushes had not: Ms. Moneybags had a forthright gaze that declared her as judge, jury, and executioner with a rare chance of absolution.

He wasn't surprised. The oldest Hirsch sister had a reputation as a no-BS businessperson, and her LuxeLinks Club was the most valuable property in her growing empire because it was shrouded in secrecy. Search engines generated results about golf courses, or The Links, a respected African-American volunteer service organization started in the mid-1900s. Hirsch's LuxeLinks Club had no digital footprint beyond one page automatically generated by the world's largest social networking site. The few details in that sparse profile were all preceded by the word allegedly. The LuxeLinks Club didn't want or need publicity.

Margeaux was very selective about approving each one of the companions, who were rumored to be hand-picked by her and her sisters. Jon respected Margeaux for building a successful career on the foundation of her personal tragedy. That respect meant he wouldn't need to fake being interested in her club during this lunch interview. It also meant that he'd feel personally disappointed if she turned out to be a high-class madam.

⁛

Margeaux watched as Uncle J. Low stood and offered his hand to Jonathan James Tiptree. Seeing that the two men looked similar in age surprised her even though she had seen a copy of the federal agent's driver's license and badge credentials. She knew that the two men's birth years differed by more than a decade, making her honorary uncle the older man.

Her legal representative turned self-appointed mentor was older, but his open face and indoorsman's pallor made him look much younger than Agent Tiptree, whose potent combination of sharp gaze, weathered skin and honed body presented the harshest picture of undiluted masculinity she'd ever seen. He appeared honed to a razor's edge by life.

"Your bosses' and your mentor's recommendations make it clear that you're the best man to have at one's side or back during a work mission, Mr. Tiptree. How does that strength and reliability translate into your personal life?" she asked in a pleasantly quiet voice after greetings and introductions were exchanged.

The federal agent held her gaze as he unbuttoned his jacket and settled into the chair directly across from Margeaux. At her side, Uncle J. Low sighed. He never interfered with her tactics despite his disagreement with her application of them. She found it an effective way to identify the drama magnets, who did not meet her criteria for suitable candidates as LuxeLinks companions.

"Call me Jon if I may call you Margeaux." He paused until she nodded her consent, then he reached into the inner pocket of his jacket and withdrew a business-sized envelope. He slid it toward her across the glass tabletop. "One joint letter from my parents and my sister. Plus two more from my oldest friends. Will you read them now or resume my interrogation, Margeaux?" he asked softly enough that the approaching server didn't hear.

They ordered then discussed innocuous topics until their entrees arrived and their server departed.

∓

Each second in her company increased Jon's admiration for his potential suspect's style of conducting business. Between delicate bites of the tasty fare, she hammered away at his motives, suitability, and expectations for being paid to escort very powerful, rich women to social events.

"I need to pay back the money I borrowed from my retirement fund when I saved my parents' home from foreclosure."

He watched her pink and white rounded fingernails tap the unopened envelope holding his personal recommendations. He chewed the last bite of his steak as he waited.

⌘⌘⌘

He was the most even-tempered LuxeLinks companion candidate Margeaux had ever interviewed. If her rapid-fire inquiries annoyed Jon, she saw no signs of it from the thoughtful way he regarded her as he finished his meal.

Margeaux was not a risk-taker. She did not act on sudden impulses. She was cautious. The calm façade of Jonathan James Tiptree tempted her to dive beneath his unflappable layers of self-confident attitude and custom-fitted, ready to wear garments. His dark eyes hinted at an emotional turbulence that she wanted to soothe, which she couldn't pursue if he was her employee.

"Jon, are you as attracted to me as I am to you?"

In the ensuing moment of anticipatory silence, Uncle J. Low patted her hand before pushing back from the table. "You don't need me here for this, Margeaux," he said as he stood. "A pleasure, Jon."

ↄ◌ↄ

Jon hoped his confusion wasn't plastered across his face as he remained seated while he shook the professorial attorney's hand. This investigation had just taken an unexpected turn.

"And if I am attracted to you, Margeaux?" he asked once they were mostly alone in the private corner of the upper terrace.

"I'll offer you a list of lucrative part-time evening and weekend opportunities from other legitimate employers who would appreciate your skills," she said.

Background information compiled by his agency's researchers discovered that finding other types of supplementary employment for the companion candidates who Margeaux rejected had turned into an unforeseen informal consulting business. Her high standards meant that even her rejects were better qualified than most of the applicants her business associates saw.

"Dating you won't prevent me from investigating you," he said. "It won't keep me from arresting you if you're running a prostitution ring, Margeaux."

❧❧

So that was what the governor's odd email to her last week about hearing rumors that Margeaux was soon departing for a paddle board tour of the Pacific Islands had been—an oblique warning for her to navigate shark infested waters with caution.

Well, accusations of pandering had dogged the LuxeLinks Club since Margeaux's first successful match. Her detractors must have gained some traction among influential circles of federal law enforcement because Jon's agency was serious about eradicating all forms of sex trafficking in the US. Their record number of indictments prosecuted into convictions proved it.

"So you're the honey stick that's going to tempt me into confessing all of my alleged crimes to you, Jon?"

He nodded once. "Yes, Margeaux, I'm the bait to lure you into lowering your guard, but if we're going to explore a personal connection, you need to let the forensic accountants from my agency examine the books for all LuxeLinks transactions. Explain discrepancies. Answer all their questions. Voluntarily offer full disclosure to clear your name."

Margeaux looked directly into the stern gaze of the beautiful man seated across from her while she reminded herself that her meticulous accounting methods, combined with the fact that she was not selling sex, mitigated her risk in agreeing to Jon's terms. Conscious awareness of herself and others was her most valuable commodity, the foundation of her soapbox and the core of her message. She was not guilty of promoting prostitution in any manner, and her copious pages of documentation would prove it.

"Yes to all of that, Jon, with the stipulation that the forensic accountants examine my records on-site in my home office in my basement in the presence of my supervising accountant."

She watched Jon reach into his inner jacket pocket and pull out his phone. He dialed before his gaze swung back up to Margeaux. "I'll set things in motion with my boss."

જાજા

An hour later, instead of catching the A train to go home to Harlem to talk to Julianna and Chloe about her deal with the feds, Margeaux was strolling among the other pedestrians, taking advantage of the perfect spring weather to enjoy the High Line.

She felt like she was floating because after Jon finished coordinating terms, dates, and times for his team to invade her residential sanctuary he had asked her to spend next Saturday with him at Oakland Beach. Just thinking about it made her happy enough to twirl a quick circle in place at the edge of the water feature installation. She closed her eyes for a slow count up to five, then back down to zero. When she opened her eyes again, the world no longer spun, but she frowned at catching a glimpse of a profile she recognized from her walk around her neighborhood earlier this morning. That made her think of the other face she had seen more than once in the past forty-eight hours. She pulled out her phone.

CHAPTER 14

"Excuse me, boss," Jon said to the woman seated next to him on the bench at Chelsea Pier when he saw Margeaux's name on his phone screen.

>*You might not trust me yet, but having 2 agents follow me is overkill.*

"Anyone on our team shadowing Ms. Hirsch, boss?"
"No, Jon. Why?"
He shook his head as he texted a reply.

>*Describe them.*

He showed Margeaux's text to his boss while he waited for more details. His boss pulled out her phone.

His phone vibrated with Margeaux's reply.

>*#1 white young woman. Late 20s? Brown eyes. Slightly buck teeth. My height. Walks like a soldier. #2 white older man...*

"Where's Ms. Hirsch right now, Jon? Uncle is not shadowing her."

Jon nodded as he resumed reading.

>*...50s? Buzzed gray hair. Blue eyes. Circuitry tattoo on his neck. 6ft+*

Jon's thumbs hustled from key to key.

>*Where are you?*

Jon was already standing as Margeaux replied. To his boss he said, "Going to meet her," as he headed toward Twelfth Avenue, texting as he walked.

>*Go directly to the gift shop. Stay in the cashier area. Their security cameras have 360 coverage. I'm coming to you. 10 mins.*

Despite his cowboy boots, Jon ran like the sprinter he'd been in high school and college.

❧

Margeaux interpreted the urgency of Jon's last text as a no, the people who were following her were not federal agents, as she made her way toward the High Line Gift Shop.

By the time she entered the cool interior, she was shaking, even though she hadn't seen either the woman or the man anywhere near her for the past several minutes.

She was already launching herself into his arms by the time Jon said, "Margeaux," in a breathless tone that matched his windblown hair, ruddy face, and disheveled clothes as he stepped inside the store. The smells of sun-warmed, starched cotton and sweaty, muscular man filled her senses when his arms closed around her.

ᑫᔑᑫᔑ

"You're safe, Margeaux." Jon managed to repeat his soft assurances while stroking the length of her back.

Margeaux's stranglehold around his waist with her face tucked against his chest transmitted each shuddering tremor and sigh from her body to his.

He shrugged out of his jacket one arm at a time, then eased free of her hug to drape it around her shoulders. "It might smell a little ripe after my run," he said as the material settled, engulfing her from neck to thighs.

He tucked her under his arm before turning them toward the exit.

"Come on, Margeaux. We're going to agency head-quarters to talk to the team."

∾∾∾

The interrogation room was open and airy with pot-ted, thriving green plants on the deep ledges in front of the oversized windows.

"If Jon is playing the good, understanding agent, then which of you is going to play bad agent?" Margeaux was looking at Jon's boss, but her question was for every federal agent in the comfortable room.

The woman in charge smiled. "Around here, it's al-ways bad agent, worst agent. Usually, Jon is our go-to hard ass of a worst nightmare agent for a suspect."

During her pause, her gaze took in Jon's seated posi-tion on the arm of Margeaux's chair with Margeaux, still swathed in his jacket, tucked against his side and leaning her closer arm along his muscular thigh while his hand cupped her opposite shoulder without disturbing the cold can of soda she was holding.

"Something about you, Ms. Hirsch, brings out his softer side." More briskly, she continued, "But that's not why you're getting the red carpet treatment today. You earned that for yourself by capturing one of your shadows on video, and by describing the other one well enough for us to identify him from our archive of baddies."

She leaned closer to Margeaux. "The woman is a coercion expert for the Wallkast Mafia of Wall Street financiers and K Street lobbyists. She convinces resistant parties to reconsider their positions by demonstrating why cooperating is in their best interests. Power tools and heavy duty tarps are often involved."

Jon gently chafed her arm a few times from shoulder to elbow when she shivered.

"The man is simply known as Hack. Liberating intellectual property claims from their inventors is his specialty.

"Ms. Hirsch, can you think of reasons why one or both of these criminals is interested in you?"

છ૩૯૩

"What do you mean, The feds have her in custody?"

The young woman resisted her desire to roll her eyes.

"I follow her from her house to NoSqua House. I wait at outdoor café across street. Follow her from lunch to High Line. I stay outside when she goes into gift shop with many surveillance cameras. Then drift away when big man who moves like a professional law enforcement officer runs in and hugs her."

Backup weapon in a sheath inside his cowboy boot at his ankle and handcuffs at his waist shouted federal agent to her, but she offered no explanations, excuses, or apologies to her employer, who cursed loudly while he paced in front of her.

"Suspend observing Margeaux Hirsch for now. I'll find out why the feds are embracing her instead of arresting her."

❧❧❧

His associates had big plans for Oyster Glen Cove, Maryland, and getting Margeaux Carr Hirsch convicted on felony pandering charges was the first step toward achieving their desired outcome.

❧❧❧

With his bicycle leaning against a trash receptacle, Hack stood across the street from the non-descript building where his target had entered—after getting out of an unmarked police cruiser—with the vigilant man who had his clothes and his arms wrapped around her.

None of the rumors about Margeaux Hirsch's invention had been verified—yet, but he felt like he was on the trail of something worth taking.

❧❧❧

"The team of forensic accounting investigators will arrive at your home at eleven a.m. tomorrow, Ms. Hirsch…"

Margeaux heard the woman's voice as if she were listening through a drinking straw filled with cotton, while thoughts about coercion experts and intellectual property liberators swirled in her overloaded brain.

Hearing, "Jon's personal involvement," switched Margeaux's concentration from internal to external focus.

Everyone in the room was staring at her and Jon in their cozy pose. When she looked up, Jon was already looking down into her face.

"As of this minute, my primary task is to protect Margeaux until we know why she's being followed." He looked toward his boss again. "Do I need to request personal leave?"

His boss shook her head.

"No. I'm changing your assignment to personal security for a material witness in an active investigation. Just complete a declaration of intent to engage personally with Ms. Hirsch and a non-disclosure pledge regarding classified information before you leave today. That should satisfy the prosecutors if charges come out of this."

They were speaking plain English, but Margeaux felt so confused. She looked up and squeezed Jon's thigh until he looked down at her again.

"What's happening, Jon?"

He hunched a little closer. "You've got yourself a live-in bodyguard as companion until further notice, Margeaux. Is that a problem for you?"

Maybe for her mind, definitely not for her body. "No, it's not," she said very softly. "What about you?"

Their foreheads were almost close enough to touch.

"Moving in with you to keep you safe is not a problem for me. At all, Margeaux."

ೞೞ

An hour later, the boss and the four other IVS core team members watched as their colleague and the potential suspect-turned-witness waited for the elevator to take them down to the garage level.

They silently observed the intimate tableau of the taller, stronger man standing with one arm draped around the shorter, more delicate woman's shoulders while in his other hand he carried his leather duffle filled with backup gear and clothes.

"Bet?" one of them asked after the couple disappeared behind the slowly closing doors of the elevator.

"Naked as soon as they get inside her house and Jon secures the premises," someone else said with sighing amusement in her voice.

"Married within the year," the agent who had worked with Jon for the longest time said.

"*What*?" the other four shouted then gathered closer together when other staff looked up from their cubicles and glanced their way.

"Has hard-assed Agent Tiptree ever comforted anyone other than rescued victims of sex trafficking or his nieces and nephews?"

Eventually, they all shook their heads as they looked at each other and smiled.

"That match is a done deal, folks."

CHAPTER 15

Feeling as if she were dreaming a very strange dream, Margeaux added her thanks to the uniformed police officer as she and Jon got out of the back seat of the unmarked sedan.

Jon already had her housekey in one hand as he herded her in front of him up the steps to her front door. His strength, his scent, his warmth surrounded her as he unlocked the door, caging her in his arms between his bigger body, his duffle over his shoulder, and the entry to her home. He tucked her key into his pants pocket.

"Give me the full tour, Margeaux.," he said after securing the ornately etched solid steel outer door and the simple wood and glass inner door.

The skylight usually kept the small space from feeling too close, but Jon's hungry look, combined with his nearness, made it difficult for her to inhale a deep breath as she reset the security alarm from vacant mode to occupied. Jon looked up at the ceiling with a frown.

"Good," he said when she told him that the skylight was wired into the security system.

She reached for his free hand and tugged him deeper into the interior of the safe haven that she and her sisters had created for themselves and their younger half-brother, Franklin.

⌘

"He's only nineteen and still lives with our dad when he's not in college, but this is his room when he's here."

Jon heard Margeaux's deep affection for her youngest sibling in her voice and marveled at the generosity of spirit that allowed her to love the offspring of the woman who had committed adultery with her father, setting off a chain of events that had ultimately led to her mother's suicide.

The young man's room was on the main floor beyond the living room, which had a mahogany concert grand piano wedged into the corner closest to the chef's kitchen leading to the dining room and media den, flanked with a half-bath on each side of the extra-wide doorway.

"Two bedrooms, each with their own shower bath on this floor," she said as he followed the provocative sway of her hips up the wide staircase to the second story.

She swept her hand toward the two doors opened onto the long hall. "Home base for Julianna and Chloe when they're not traveling."

He checked the locks on every window just as he had in the basement and on the main floor.

"Where are your sisters tonight, Margeaux?"

He followed her to an alcove at the end of the hall.

"While I was waiting for you in the gift shop I texted them to go stay with Dad tonight."

"Good," he said as they ascended a very narrow set of stairs to the third floor. "Are they the ones who've been blowing up your phone for the past hour?"

Margeaux laughed. "Oh, yeah. My last 'everything's going to be fine' text to them was hours ago."

Jon followed when she stepped through an open door and into a big space with a wall of windows lined up like framed works of art on the back wall.

"Opaque from the outside and bulletproof," she said before he could ask. "This was originally four small rooms for servants. We opened it up into one large living space with a full bath and a kitchenette."

Jon approved. Of the woman, her inviting home, and her security measures. He dropped his duffle bag to the wide border of hardwood floor that framed the luxuriously thick area rug. He said, "Why don't you call your sisters while I run down to lock the pocket door that seals off the upper floors from the main floor. Okay?"

"Okay."

Jon forced himself to turn away from the temptation of her allure from the top of her shiny disheveled curls that made his fingers itch to snare them, to her solemn brown eyes, tender lips, and softly rounded chin.

His final glimpse of the double-take appeal of her body and her showgirl's legs subtly displayed to great advantage in a romantic dress under a simple pale green cardigan hounded his good intentions all the way down the narrow flight of stairs.

⌇⌇

"No! Don't come home tonight or tomorrow," Margeaux said to her sisters on their three-way cell connection. "I'm fine. Agent Tiptree is temporarily moving in to keep me safe."

"Who is Agent Tiptree?" Julianna asked at the same time Chloe said, "I hope he's single, hetero, and sexy."

Margeaux heard Jon's rapidly approaching footsteps.

"I'll explain everything when we come for dinner at Dad's tomorrow night. I need to go. I love you both. Goodbye!" she said then ended the call while they kept trying to interrogate her.

Margeaux turned and tossed her phone on top of her dressing table as Jon stepped into the room. Physically, he was big and dark and hard. His face remained stern even while he was patiently offering her comfort, but seeing him and being with him made her feel lighthearted with giddiness. Safe. And very sexy.

"What time is dinner at your dad's tomorrow?"

She didn't answer immediately because her whole focus was on savoring the pleasure of watching him prowl over to her bedside table while shrugging out of his jacket and tossing it to drape across one of the matching armchairs upholstered in black and white toile before he methodically removed his shoulder holster, his handcuffs, and his ankle sheath and holster.

He pointed at the closed bottom drawer. "May I?" he asked.

She nodded.

Watching him kneel to store the tools of his trade kept her silent until he stood and moved to within touching distance.

"Drinks at seven; first course at seven-thirty."

She reached up to start unbuttoning his wilted dress shirt. His hands gently captured hers, holding them still.

"Margeaux," he said.

When she looked up directly into his eyes his piercing focus compelled her to hold his serious gaze.

"Be very sure that I'm the only man you want in your bed. Inside your body. Because I want all of you, Margeaux—body and soul—for however long we last."

He cupped her hands in his rough palms before sliding his palms over her wrists and up her forearms, making her shiver in response to the chaste caress muted by the fine layer of the cashmere sleeves of her cardigan. The tips of his fingers stroked up over her elbows then coasted across the back of her upper arms until his palms rested lightly atop her shoulders. He leaned down.

"We met each other for the first time at one o'clock this afternoon." He glanced at his dive watch. "It's now eight-forty-seven. Are you sure I'm the man you want, Margeaux? Because I'll protect you from the bad guys no matter what—even if we never become friends or lovers."

Snippets about Jon's integrity and reliability from his three professional references popped into her head, but it was the group letter from his immediate family that touched her the most when she'd finally read it while in the ladies room at the agency headquarters. Each adult had written one paragraph about why they loved Jon. Both parents offered examples of his considerate actions as a dutiful son. His sister praised his financial generosity, and his patience with her four rowdy children, who had each added one sentence about their only uncle.

The youngest, four-year-old Bruce, had written in blue crayon, *Unkl Jon plaz fun an hugs good 2.*

Impulsive decisions weren't her thing. Prior to today, she couldn't remember her last impulsive act. For once, she was not going to worry about tomorrow, next week, next month, or next year. She was going to accept everything Jon was offering at this moment.

She resumed unbuttoning his dress shirt.

"There's a box of condoms in the top dresser drawer."

A slight hitch in Jon's breathing was the only outward sign that she had surprised him with her reply.

"Kisses first, Margeaux. I've been fantasizing about your mouth since one o'clock this afternoon."

A fraction of a second later, she went from standing in front of Jon with her fingers slipping the last button free on his shirt to reveal a white ribbed tank undershirt stretched over his muscular chest and taut waist, to being seated across his lap once he lowered his truly impressive butt onto the tufted bench at the foot of her bed.

The first touch of his closed lips against hers teased her with a glancing drag from one corner of her mouth to the other and continued up over her cheekbone to her ear. Her whole body shivered at the feel of his warm breath.

"Tonight is for kissing until we both come, Margeaux," he whispered. His nibbling tugs on her earlobe made her laugh and squirm in his secure embrace. He chuckled softly. "I wonder where else you're ticklish."

Margeaux grabbed his face and laid her lips to his with enough pressure to part the seam and lick the tender inside of his lips with the tip of her tongue.

∽∾∽∾

Jon may have miscalculated in thinking that just kissing would support his good intentions toward waiting until at least tomorrow night before plunging his dick into Margeaux's irresistible body cozied up on his lap. Every time she moved her ass, the full round globes of supple flesh rubbed against his very hard dick.

He wanted her. He wanted her right now. And her insistent forays between his lips with her tongue brushing side to side across the sensitive skin of his inner lips and teeth were not helping him to control his urge to pull her astride his crotch for a deep, hard ride.

He opened his mouth to coax her tongue deeper. While her hands clutched at his ears, his hands started removing her clothes. Working her cropped knit cardigan off her shoulders was easy compared to getting Margeaux to release him, one ear at a time, to let him work the clingy material down and off of her arms before tackling the row of tiny buttons down the front of her sleeveless dress.

She moaned in complaint when he pulled back to break their mouth to mouth connection.

"Margeaux."

Her eyelids very slowly drifted up.

"Unbutton your dress for me."

She blinked. Her tight grip on his ears gradually loosened. Her fingers straightened, stroking down the side of his face and his jaw, before she pulled her hands away from his face and started easily unbuttoning the front of her dress.

The bright emerald green lace of her bra was a surprising revelation. He smiled into her eyes.

"Beautiful, Margeaux."

Jon lowered his head until they were close enough to resume their kissing agenda.

☙❧

Seeing the brilliance of his smile for the first time shocked Margeaux into docile acceptance of the barely there press of his lips on hers like a phantom weight from memory of their earlier kisses. She ached for more.

She felt his lips curve against hers as she hugged him closer, deepening their kiss into an ebb and flow of suckling tongues and lips, filling her head with another wave of the potent mélange of his scent.

She twisted her whole body into their kiss, rubbing her lace covered breasts against his chest at the same time she squeezed her thighs together and swiveled her butt across his deliciously hard erection.

"Let's do more than kiss, Jon." She rotated her hips into a grind that made him toss his head back with an ecstatic groan. "I know you want more," she said.

Margeaux became the source of ecstatic sighs when Jon lowered his head to trail kisses down the length of her neck, across her chest and over the swells of her breasts pushed up by the full cups of her lacy bra.

He lingered at her cleavage, licking the divide of her mounded flesh, then delving even deeper with the tip of his tongue in a repetitive loop that drove her crazy with wanting more. Her nipples ached, and so did her clitoris.

She cried out her frustration when he lifted his face from her breasts.

"You're right, Margeaux, I do want more. I want to see all of you. I want to kiss all of you. Will you let me?"

"Yes."

℘℘℘

"Yes!" she screamed an hour later when Jon had her completely naked on her back in the middle of her destroyed bed.

The entire surface of her skin vibrated from the frequency of being licked and stroked and suckled and nipped by Jon's tongue and his lips and his mouth and teeth. She felt as if her bruising grip around the back of her thighs, holding her own legs folded back along the sides of her torso, was the only anchor keeping her from flying apart while Jon filled her vagina with his tongue and two fingers thrusting hard and deep in concert with the prod of his nose against her clitoris.

The unexpected forceful insertion of one of his thick, rough fingers into her clenched rectum shoved her over the edge into a sobbing, screaming orgasm.

℘℘℘

Her cunt and her asshole locked down on Jon's tongue and his fingers, making him work harder to keep pumping her as she creamed all over his face and hand.

Slowly, gently, he stopped moving. He waited until her cries subsided and her internal muscles relaxed enough for him to withdraw his tongue and his fingers.

Without taking his eyes off the visual spectacle of Margeaux's carnal bounty, Jon reached behind his back for his discarded tank shirt and wiped his face before tossing the shirt aside to roll on one of the condoms from his supply in his duffle bag.

Watching Margeaux's open mouth gasping for breath, the rise and fall of her gorgeous breasts glistening with sweat, the soft swell of her taut stomach, her mound, her clit, and the plump folds of her engorged cunt lips, still weeping her response, battered at his reasons for not immediately sliding his dick balls-deep into the sexual nirvana of her tight sheath.

After inhaling several deep breaths, Jon reached forward and pushed her bent legs together from thighs to knees to ankles, creating a narrow crevice above her sex. He laid his covered dick from root to tip along the juicy petals of her slit, sliding back and forth from the slap of his balls against her ass to the nudge of his tip, against her clit, as he thrust between her soft thighs without penetrating her.

"Yeah, Margeaux, look at me," he said when she opened her eyes and watched him through a veil of drowsy vagueness even as she moaned and tilted her ass to meet his pumping thrusts.

ೞ

Each thrust tightened her vaginal muscles in anticipation of being stretched and filled, jolting her senses when her sex remained empty while her clitoris kept getting stimulated at the end of every stroke.

This time, taking his finger into her rectum didn't surprise her, and there was more room for accepting it with an empty vagina. The forceful addition of a second finger drew a high-pitched cry from her, which instantly halted all motion in Jon's body.

"Too much?" he asked.

While Jon's strong body vibrated with the exertion of forcing himself to remain still, Margeaux listened to her body. After a moment, she said, "Two fingers are enough."

Jon nodded, then started pumping his hips and fingers in a steady rhythm of opposing thrusts and withdrawals, which he sustained through her next two orgasms until he finally came with a roaring cry of her name before he collapsed at her side and half sprawled across her.

They gasped together for what felt like a long time.

"How are you walking around single in New York City, Jon?" she finally found the breath and energy to ask as she watched him remove the condom, tie it off, wrap it in tissues from the baroque silver dispenser on the bedside table, then drop it into the decorative metal trash bin next to her bed.

He tossed dirty clothes, underwear, one of her shoes, and empty condom wrappers off the mattress, got back into bed, and angled the top sheet up to cover her from the shoulders down while his half of the sheet settled at his waist before he answered.

Jon lay on his side with his head propped against the palm of his hand. Margeaux looked up at him from lying flat on her back.

"I work a lot. I work odd hours. If I'm not working, I'm with my family when I'm not at the shooting range or hand combat training." He must have read the speculation on her face because he said, "No, I don't date coworkers—too messy. I learned that my first year as an agent."

He glanced over at the small vintage mantel clock on her bedside table.

"It's getting late, Margeaux. Today was long and exhausting. Tomorrow will be longer." He leaned down to press his smiling lips to hers. "Wake me if I'm still asleep when you get up. My new lover tried to wear me out tonight."

Margeaux laughed. "I'm the one who's prostrate from your extended foreplay, Jon. I get up at five-thirty to belly dance. Should I wake you after my workout?"

His dark eyes twinkled with interest as he shook his head. "Oh, no, please be sure to wake me before your workout," he said, sliding down onto his stomach and throwing his arm across her stomach to pull her closer.

Once they were settled, Margeaux extended her arm toward the lamp on her bedside table and tapped its base with her fingertip, plunging the room into darkness.

"Cool," he said sleepily.

"Thanks."

"You're welcome."

∽∾∽

In the morning, Margeaux used her mouth to wake Jon, who shouted his appreciation as she drank him dry, then he turned her belly dancing workout into a contact sport.

They showered together and dressed in time to finish eating the sumptuous breakfast that Jon made two hours before the forensic accountants descended upon them and dampened their post-orgasmic buzz.

∽∾∽

"I still can't believe it, Jon," the most senior forensic accountant on the team of four said. "I didn't think anyone used old-fashioned ledgers anymore. Certainly no one under the age of forty."

Jon agreed. Finding out that Margeaux recorded every transaction for the LuxeLinks Club in the ledger books rigged with a triple binding and carbon paper system, which allowed her to make three simultaneous copies of each entry and to separate the original ledger from the duplicates with the flip of a single compression lever sounded like labor intensive throwbacks to a time before computers. Her manual receipt book also used primitive-tech carbon paper, which totally contradicted the word processing software and Braille printer she had in order to make it easier for her unnamed good friend from college to read her weekly letters to him since being blinded five years ago.

Without looking up from where she was seated in the corner working on her laptop, Margeaux said, "All documents related to the LuxeLinks Club members and companions are off-line. No emails. Nothing hackable. I guarantee that the specific terms of their involvement will remain private. The required government forms and tax filings are the only digital footprints for the club."

Still feeling mellow from the best wake-up sex of his life, and a stomach full of delicious food, Jon observed Margeaux's diligent focus while the investigators sifted through her account books. On-premises examination and no photographing, copying or scanning of her documents were the non-negotiable terms of her voluntary cooperation.

"What are you working on, Margeaux?"

Her fingers stopped tapping the keyboard, and she looked up. "Final authorizations before the grand opening of the LuxeLinks Beach Club in Oyster Glen Cove, Maryland, in three weeks."

"You and your sisters inherited that land from your mother, right?"

Margeaux nodded. "Yes, it was an environmental dead zone she purchased from the US Bureau of Land Management in the 1980s after some heroine and meth dealers sank a boat filled with finished product and raw chemicals for producing tons more. Some of the water remained spontaneously flammable for almost a year. My mom let environmental conservationists experiment on the area with their habitat recovery…"

She finished with, "The terms of the sale require the US Government to reimburse the Carr Family Trust for ten times the current market value if it uses eminent domain or national security concerns to reclaim the property and water rights. She believed that the land would recover eventually. My mom was as savvy in business as she was naïve with romance."

The most senior forensic accountant said what Jon was thinking. "I know what the Wallkast Mafia wants from you."

When another investigative accountant tried to sneak some pictures of her ledger pages with his cell phone Margeaux said, "It won't work, sir. The light in here whites out the images."

Her calm statement generated blushing apologies from the investigator and questions from Jon and the lead accountant.

Two hours later, Jon summarized, "In addition to light bulbs that prevent photographs from displaying, your youngest siblings, Chloe and Franklin, also invented the photostatic reflective printer ink you use for all your contracts with LuxeLinks Club members and companions because then the documents cannot be photocopied, scanned, faxed or photographed. That's why you conduct LuxeLinks business in-person and by messenger service." That last thought clarified his understanding of why she'd included three copies of the companion agreement in the sample packet she'd allowed them to examine. "You, the club member, and the companion sign and date all three copies, and each of you keeps one for your own records."

Margeaux nodded. "Even if people violate the non-disclosure clause by showing the contract to someone outside of LuxeLinks, they can't broadcast the original documents through mass media platforms. They could physically post it in a public place, but no one would be able to snap a viewable picture of it."

Jon considered the obvious possible political, military, and espionage applications.

"This ink is what Hack wants from you, Margeaux."

CHAPTER 16

Jon glanced down at the sleeping woman seated next to him in the back seat of the armored SUV. Two agents he'd worked with on other cases were in the front seats. The driver's specialty was financial services crimes, and the other man's was intellectual property theft, particularly high-tech.

Printer ink was very low tech, but the Hirsch siblings' version was sophisticated enough to circumvent high-tech devices, which made it relevant to national security according to Uncle Sam.

They were only ten minutes out from arriving at John Snelling Hirsch's New York City suburban mansion in North Salem for explanations, drinks, and dinner.

Margeaux's eyelids fluttered heavily until she forced them to stay up. Tinted windows darkened the car interior and her view of the countryside at dusk.

She felt the weight of Jon's regard and looked up at him.

"Did the power nap help?"

"Yes, it really did, Jon," she said, leaning away from him to stretch and shake off the tension creeping back into her shoulders.

She and LuxeLinks were in the clear, she reminded herself. The forensic accounting investigators had been impressed with how accurately her triplicated handwritten ledgers were when verified by the files from her bank, her financial advisor, and the IRS. Everyone, except Jon, had packed up and left her home an hour before their departure for dinner. Jon's boss was using the unlikely possibility that the Wallkast Mafia wanted to use Oyster Glen Cove to smuggle human cargo into the Mid-Atlantic region as justification for keeping Jon assigned to Margeaux, which Margeaux greatly appreciated.

"It's going to be okay, Margeaux." He spoke softly while watching her blot her face, fluff her curls, and tug at the bodice of her clingy, lightweight knit dress.

"You said the patent and trademark documents are filed under the Carr Family Trust. Since you're the oldest and the publicly known entrepreneur, Margeaux, these interested parties are assuming you're the inventor. They've dismissed Julianna, the concert pianist; Chloe, the professional outdoor adventure thrill seeker; and Franklin, who's only nineteen now—sixteen when he and Chloe perfected their ideas. Those factors keep them safe and give us a strategic advantage. We're just going to warn your family to pay attention to their surroundings and exercise basic common sense."

୧୨୧୨

There was an armed guard in each of the booths that flanked the heavy metal gate at the bottom of the winding driveway.

"Good evening, Ms. Hirsch," said the guard who approached when the driver lowered his window once he'd leaned forward to conduct a visual inspection of everyone inside the vehicle. "It's good to see you, miss."

"It's good to be seen, Phil," Margeaux said.

Jon knew from Margeaux's earlier briefing while they were getting dressed that saying, "Thanks. You, too," would have alerted the guards to a serious problem worthy of police intervention. She'd also shared that tech in the guard booths and in the ground under the vehicle was scanning for tracking devices, biotoxins, and explosives.

The gate started sliding open when the first guard signaled the other one. He stepped back and waved them forward once the gate was fully retracted.

Jon wasn't easily impressed, but the closer they drove to Margeaux's father's mansion, the more impressed he became. It was a jewel of architectural splendor at the center of a lush setting of exotic manicured lawns. A uniformed staff member opened the back door for Margeaux when the car stopped in front of a sweeping fan of gray marble steps leading to ornately carved double doors.

Jon scooped his arms under her hips to lift her up and out with him as he slid them both out of the car on her side. He leaned down to whisper in her ear after he set her on her feet. "You're even farther out of my league than I originally thought, Margeaux. Are you slumming with me?"

Margeaux stepped into his body, tipping her head all the way back to look up into his stern gaze. "You're a hard-working, generous, honorable, ethical man, Jon. You're about to find out that you're the one who's slumming."

He watched her pivot and straighten her shoulders as if she was bracing herself for a battle as she greeted the staff by name on her graceful march up the stairs, through the doors, and into the residential showplace.

෴

"Sweetheart M.!" Strong arms gathered her in. "Sweetheart J. and Sweetheart C. are in the music room with your father and Ms. Duchamp."

Margeaux sank into Mrs. Brown's pillowy hug, absorbing her love and concern with each deep inhale of the older woman's comforting scent of floral notes, spices, and extracts.

Margeaux gently pulled back from the loving embrace. "Mrs. Brown, let me introduce Agent Jonathan Tiptree and the other agents who are coordinating their investigation..."

Mrs. Brown herded them into the first room off the wide corridor, as receiving area, before she allowed Margeaux to introduce her entourage to everyone who turned away from the patent black concert grand piano in the center of the room.

"Now that's everyone." Mrs. Brown clapped her soft hands together then slowly backed out of the room. From the corridor, she said, "Open these doors when the business chat is done, and I'll start the dinner service, Mr. Hirsch." She pulled the glass doors shut.

"Well, don't just stand there. Have a drink. What's your pleasure, Margeaux? Agents?" Her dad's voice sing-songed with the affable cadence of the superficially cheerful, functional drunk he had become since the death of his second wife, Franca Milne Hirsch, in a car accident a year ago.

Across the room, Chloe's gaze caught Margeaux's eye, then her baby sister mimicked tossing back a few drinks while Julianna started playing a Chopin sonata, her go-to composer as an anti-anxiety soother.

Catherine Duchamp, the exquisitely beautiful, obscenely wealthy tech entrepreneur jonesing to be Mrs. Hirsch number three looked very concerned about Margeaux's dad. Margeaux wished the truly lovely genius would consider getting to know a few of the LuxeLinks companions.

"*What*? Am I surrounded by pansy-assed teetotalers?" her dad groused.

Margeaux sighed in her head. Just another weekly family dinner at the Hirsch estate.

⌘⌘⌘

So many pieces clicked into place for Jon about Margeaux's family dynamics as he observed them, while the other two agents took turns summarizing different aspects of the situation.

John Snelling Hirsch was a distinguished-looking senior gentleman with a charming smile. He asked surprisingly coherent questions about his children's safety, and he slowed the pace of his alcohol consumption.

The younger Hirsch sisters promised Margeaux that they wouldn't go places alone or walk around distracted by their personal tech devices.

Catherine Duchamp wanted to discuss the commercial applications of Chloe and Franklin's inventions with Chloe since the youngest Hirsch was away at college.

Everyone agreed with Margeaux's suggestion to wait until after his last final exam of the semester to share details with Franklin before he headed off to Nepal as a humanitarian aid volunteer for most of the summer.

Margeaux was the calm eye of this family's stormy undercurrents.

Mrs. Brown acted as much as their mother as she was their house manager and drill sergeant. She clearly loved them all, but Margeaux was her favorite while Mr. Hirsch was her biggest concern.

❧❧❧

Three dinner courses and one dessert course later, Mrs. Brown was urging Margeaux and Jon and the other agents to spend the night.

"Thank you, Mrs. Brown, for the invitation to stay and for the charming evening. Your meal was the best tasting homecooked food I've ever eaten." Still seated, Jon leaned closer to the Hirsch house manager as she stood next to his chair. "Please don't tell my mom I said that."

Mrs. Brown chuckled and stepped back when Jon pushed away from the table to stand.

"The other agents and I need to return to the city tonight, but if Julianna and Chloe could stay here until the beginning of next week, that would streamline security coverage." Jon kept talking, reminding everyone of points from their pre-dinner discussion as he helped Margeaux from her dining chair.

"The article about the grand opening of the LuxeLinks Beach Club goes live on the newspaper's site at three a.m. Sunday with bonus content to support the print article in the business section. Once the general terms of the Oyster Glen Cove land contracts become public knowledge, the Wallkast Mafia should lose interest.

"Margeaux has an appointment with a rep from R and D at the US Department of Defense on Monday, which should eliminate any potential threats from Hack.

"It's Wednesday night so," Jon swept his gaze over the people still seated at the massive rectangular banquet table while Margeaux stood at his side and the other two agents stood at his back in preparation for their departure. "Julianna and Chloe, if you'd make North Salem your home base for the next week that would help us focus on keeping your sister safe until we're sure she's in the clear."

∽∾∽∾∽

Margeaux admired Jon's slick way of using her sisters' concern for her safety as leverage to get Julianna and Chloe to agree to stay with their dad.

After only three hours, Jon had identified the most expedient manner of incentivizing her sisters' cooperation and easing her worries about their safety.

Now she just wanted to go home with Jon to continue their carnal explorations.

⊱⊰

Twenty minutes later, with arms laden with canvas tote bags filled with leftovers in fancy containers, Jon finally got them out the front door and into the armored SUV after more hugs and scoldings to be careful from Mrs. Brown and Margeaux's sisters.

"Sleep," he said when Margeaux wilted against him in the back seat, tugging until she lay on her side with her head on his thigh.

⊱⊰

Being lifted woke Margeaux halfway. Being juggled between a hard door and a hard body while the hand under her thighs worked the lock open, completely awakened her as Jon whispered thanks and goodnights to the other two agents before he carried her and their bags of leftovers inside and shut the door.

"Awake enough to stand, Margeaux?" he asked softly when she managed to raise her heavy eyelids.

She nodded, then felt her legs slowly lowered until her shoes tapped the floor. Jon kept his arm around her waist while he opened the inner door, then watched her reset the security alarm mode.

He gently cupped her face between the rough palms of his big hands and gazed directly into her eyes.

"Are you too tired, Margeaux?"

She grabbed the lapels of his jacket to help her pull his mouth down to hers. "No, Jon, I'm not tired at all," she murmured against his lips before she kissed him.

CHAPTER 17

Margeaux was getting addicted to kissing Jon. His repertoire of kisses was vast and deep, sometimes shallow, always tantalizing to all of her senses.

Kissing him while sitting naked astride his lap as the broad head of his substantial erection brushed her clitoris with enough force to make her jerk and cry out against his greedy mouth before his tight grip on her butt guided her lower, breaching the folds of her labia and stretching her sopping wet vagina to accommodate his length and breadth, stuffing her full to bursting from the mouth of her womb to his balls overloaded her ability to care about anything other than orgasms for herself and for him.

She pressed her palms atop his strong shoulders to brace herself to fight the restraint of his grappling hold on her butt. She flexed, using her glutes and her thighs to work her sex up and down his hard penis while she ate at his lips and suckled his tongue, transforming their kiss into a seductive battle neither one of them lost.

ᵒᴐᵉᴐ

Jon let go.

The hot wet invitation of her mouth and her tongue echoed the damp clutch of her tight cunt scorching the length of his dick. He needed more hands and another mouth to suck and fondle and caress her everywhere he wanted to claim her body as exclusively his to pleasure and to protect.

He slid his hands from her very fine ass to her waist, supporting her position as her increasingly frantic up and down motions undercut her stability astride his groin and dragged her jiggling breasts against his upper chest. Sucking on her pointy nipples became an urgent compulsion.

ᵒᴐᵉᴐ

"Come back," Margeaux said when Jon dragged his lips away from her mouth to nibble kisses down her rounded chin, across her jaw to her ear.

She arched her neck and moaned when his teeth tugged at her earlobe. The involuntary grinding swivel of her hips lodged him deeper and stretched her almost more than she could bear.

On the next upstroke, his lips trailed down the side of her neck while his arm cinched her waist across her back, arching her forward and putting her breasts in the perfect spot for his descending mouth to capture one of her sensitive nipples.

Clamped into place by Jon's lips at her breast, the unyielding down and in pressure of his arm at her back, and his thickening erection staked between her legs, Margeaux submitted her whole self to all of the overwhelming pleasure of taking Jon into her body and letting go in his arms.

His free hand worked between their plastered together bodies to stroke her slippery clitoris with the rough pad of one fingertip.

She felt his lips curve into a smile against her breast as she spiraled into orgasm.

∽∾∽

Margeaux stiffened and screamed in Jon's arms. His ears drank in every high-pitched to guttural note.

She struggled to move against his inescapable embrace. Her delicate fists pounded his shoulders off the beat of the squeeze and release in her juicy, quivering cunt. He surrendered and savored every tactile link that bound him tighter to this fascinating woman.

❦

"I can't believe you're eating a full meal at two o'clock in the morning, Jon."

From her comfortable sprawl on the wrecked bed, Margeaux watched him standing in all his naked glory as he arranged an assortment of leftovers from the containers he'd stuffed into the little refrigerator under the countertop in her kitchenette.

"We'll burn it off during naked belly dancing in a few hours, and I can't believe you and your sisters aren't morbidly obese."

Margeaux laughed. "Mrs. Brown is a firm believer in portion control, long nature walks, and shooing children outside to play until it's time for them to wash their hands for dinner."

She scooted closer to the headboard to make room for Jon and his smorgasbord. "Plus, Dad asks her to make Wednesday family dinners extra special since Franca's death last year," she said, keeping her eyes cast down toward the food on the tray Jon placed between them on the mattress.

"Do you want to talk about your dad's drinking, Margeaux?"

No. She didn't want to talk about it, but she wanted Jon to understand the basics.

"His heavy drinking started the night we buried Franca. Before that, he was a very moderate social drinker. Con artists always need their wits unimpaired in case the game goes sideways."

"Grief counseling?"

She shrugged. "He arranged it for us as children after our mom died, but claims real men just lock it down and move forward. These days most of his duties for the Hirsch Department Stores are social in nature: entertaining, ego-stroking, glad-handing majority shareholders, politicians, labor union officials, and venture capitalists.

"My dad was a good husband to Franca because she always saw him for who he really was. She had no illusions about his character. I'm pretty sure he was faithful to her—or at least he was discreet, unlike his behavior with my mom." Margeaux still remembered her parents' fights. The yelling. The crying. Both only partially muffled behind their closed bedroom door.

∽∾∽∾

Jon recognized the burden of that knowledge in Margeaux's eyes and in the flat tone of her voice.

"What kind of dad was he when you were little?" he asked.

"The best kind: loving, attentive, playful, and really patient, especially when all four of us were competing for his time. He's not a monster. He's not evil. His parents chose my mom for him because she was a wealthy, docile, orphaned heiress who could restore them to the social standing previous generations of their family had enjoyed before the stock market crash reduced their number of stores from thirty-one to four.

"My parents' marriage was a business transaction, but my mom didn't know the truth of it until three children and years of tears later. When he left her, he took tens of millions of dollars and her pride. Julianna, Chloe, and I couldn't love her enough to make up for what he took."

Margeaux had just shared more of her emotional history with Jon, after knowing him for less than forty-eight hours, than she had revealed to previous long-term boyfriends. If Jon was planning to bag and run, she wanted him to do it now rather than later. She was already enjoying sharing meals, conversation, and a bed with him too much.

❧❧❧

Jon chewed and swallowed, never dropping his gaze from the pensive expression in Margeaux's solemn judge and jury eyes. She'd thrown down her gauntlet and he was man enough to meet her challenge. He picked up one of her hands.

"Do you know why I can't wait for this personal security assignment with you to end, Margeaux?"

She shook her head.

"Because I cannot wait to begin courting you the

way a proper gentleman should pursue a phenomenal woman like you. I cannot wait to reschedule our day at Oakland Beach, Margeaux. I want you to know me. I want to be known by you. Okay?"

"Okay."

☙❧❧

Early Sunday morning, the older man whose self-deputized mission in life was to take America back to the golden age of its traditional socio-political hierarchy tossed the business section of the newspaper on his Hepplewhite dining table.

"You said your associates at Wallkast wanted Oyster Glen Cove. You said they would do anything to get it away from that abomination of womanhood, Margeaux Carr Hirsch.

"Do they fear her?"

The younger man paused in case his mentor in the proper philosophy of life had more demands.

"Their retreat isn't based on fear. It's the irrevocable terms of the land deal. Camilla Marie Carr negotiated a hell of an ironclad deal."

"You mean her attorneys did, because there's no way that deal is a woman's work, much less the work of one who killed herself over a failed romance."

"It's her voice on the audio tapes from the meetings."

"So she memorized what her attorneys told her to

say." The older man waved away the issue with a flick of his liver-spotted hand. "And the notorious Hack's excuses are…"

The younger man kept his annoyed sigh to himself. He said, "Now that the DOD's interested in Miss Hirsch, Hack is out. Uncle Sam's already got a hard-on for him after he infiltrated the Pentagon's internal e-mail system last year. Telling them how he did it and how to prevent someone else from doing it again saved him once. He'd rather not spend the rest of his life in Leavenworth."

"That's what's wrong with you young people today. You're unwilling to suffer for your beliefs. My generation understood real sacrifice."

The younger man watched his mentor glance at the eighteen-karat-gold watch on his wrist before he impatiently gestured for the hovering servant to refill his china coffee cup, one of a set of the surviving twelve from an imported banquet service one of his ancestors had saved from being taken or destroyed by the Union Army.

⁓⁓

On Monday night, Margeaux touched the silk necktie covering her eyes and knotted at the side of her head to allow her to sit comfortably in the front passenger seat of Jon's plain gray government sedan.

"Are we there yet?" she asked when the car slowed and turned.

"Almost," Jon said. "Don't peek."

Minutes later when the car rolled to a gradual stop, Margeaux heard Jon's seat belt click and felt him turn toward her before his hand covered hers on the armrest.

"Before you take off the blindfold, Margeaux, I want to thank you for trusting me to keep you and your family safe. Thank you for letting me into your home and for taking me into your body.

"Now that other agencies are handling the closing of your case, I've brought you to my home for our first date as simply a man and a woman who are intrigued with each other."

⌀⌀⌀

Margeaux loosened the necktie enough for it to slide over her nose, down her chin to her neck. Jon's twinkling eyes didn't match his unsmiling mouth, but this particular expression of his had become familiar and dear to her during the past week. She leaned closer and pressed a chaste kiss to the stern line of his lips, which curved slightly upward from the pressure.

She pulled back and turned to take her first look through the front windshield at Jon's home.

"Oh, Jon, how charming!" she said, releasing her seat belt, then the door and popping out of the car.

⌀⌀⌀

Jon reached across the now empty space to pull Margeaux's door completely closed before he got out to join her in his miniscule front yard.

Her enthusiasm for his modest two-bedroom cottage pleased him more than he'd imagined it would.

"The yellow window awnings look so cheerful and must keep the interior cool in the summer…"

Jon smiled as he listened to her self-guided tour of the exterior of the little house he'd inherited from his dad's older brother, who never married or had kids.

"…a properly anchored carport. Probably added in the nineteen sixties when the last of the commuter servants for the historic Scarsdale mansions died or sold out to a planned community developer who went to federal prison for tax evasion before he could execute his vision.

"The state auctioned off the two dozen homes."

"Yes, that's when my dad's older brother bought it," Jon said as he caught her hand to help Margeaux keep her balance on the stone pavers that curved around the side of the house to the unfenced back yard.

"Why do you know so much about it?"

"From my mom. She studied all kinds of land deals for ideas about what works where, when, and why or why not.

"Her great-grandfather made millions from strip-mining land. She was interested in environmentally sustainable ways to generate profit."

"She sounds really intelligent."

"She was, Jon. My mom was smart and fun. She cuddled and kissed us while she hugged us. She was a loving mother and a good person."

"I believe you, Margeaux."

CHAPTER 18

Margeaux let Jon lead her around the other side of the house to the front door.

"Oh, Jon."

It wasn't just the clean lines of the sturdy furniture, oak floors, plaster walls, and crown molding at the ceilings that impressed her. It was her clear view of a bistro table in the sunny kitchen. Each step closer revealed more details to support the scents of baked bread, vegetables, and roasted meat.

"How are you cooking lamb and side dishes in your home when you've been with me since last Tuesday, Jon?"

"My mom and my sister," he said as they stepped close enough to touch the glassware, utensils, china, and linens on the beautifully set table for two. A sheet of yellow construction paper with menu items written in crayon drew their notice at the same time. Jon added, "My nieces and nephews, too."

They laughed together before turning toward the sink to wash their hands.

സൗ

"Food as foreplay—an effective classic for many good reasons, Jon."

Margeaux panted for breath under the weight and heat of Jon's sweaty body sprawled atop her. The flex of his hips nudged his semi-erect penis against the tender flesh of her sex and made her sigh.

She playfully thumped his shoulder.

"You may be a sex deity in human form, Jon, but I'm a mere mortal who needs an intermission before our next act."

"Me, too," he mumbled against her neck. "Your pussy is like an erectile over-performance drug for my dick."

"Sweet-talker."

"Plus, I can recover while you're in Maryland for the grand opening of the LuxeLinks Beach Club if you're still sure you don't want me to come with you."

"I want you there with me, Jon. It's just that I'll be so busy juggling the expectations of the charter members and a thousand other details at once. Don't burn up your paid leave for that. Save it for the romantic trip you want us to take in the fall.

"Every member of the beach club security team has been thoroughly vetted and trained by Alexa Spencer's chief of security at her company. I promise I'll be safe."

ೞೞೞ

There were aspects of Jon's personality and priorities that Margeaux understood intuitively after knowing him for only a week that had taken his coworkers and few close friends years to grasp.

He should feel spooked by that fact, but he wasn't. He was anxious to make the most of tonight before he had to drive her back, to her home, so she could finish preparing to catch her flight to Maryland tomorrow afternoon.

Jon shifted and pushed up on his forearms to look down into her sleepy eyes.

"Let me do one more thing to make sure you don't forget me while you're away."

"Odds are I wouldn't forget you, Jon, even if I had amnesia."

"Well, it never hurts to stack the deck in my favor."

CHAPTER 19
EPILOGUE

Thirteen Months Later:

Jon's coworkers sat clustered around a table wedged into the corner of the outdoor deck of the waterfront Oakland Beach pub, where family and friends of Margeaux and Jon were into hour three of dancing, drinking, and eating to celebrate the couple's engagement.

"I called it," said the agent who had worked with Jon for the longest time.

"Did not. You said married within a year."

"As good as—Tree just kept living with her after his personal security assignment ended. He staked out his territorial claim and had Margeaux locked down in under a month."

"True, but still no bragging rights for you. Let's sit back and drink another toast to love's habit of beating the odds."

CHAPTER 20

This Mark Leaps Into the Abyss
The LuxeLinks Club Story 3

Twenty Years Ago:

Seated in the plush comfort of his ergonomically designed executive chair, family trust and estate planning attorney Jaime Lowenthal waited for the oldest Hirsch sister to challenge his answer to her earlier question. Her perch atop his oversized desk put her at eye level with him and with her chaperone, Mrs. Brown, who was seated in a visitor's chair pulled close to one side of his desk.

"But how do you know my daddy won't stop loving me, and my sisters, like he stopped loving my mommy, Uncle J. Lo?"

His peripheral vision caught the brief quirk of Mrs. Brown's lips at hearing the affectionate nickname for him in honor of the two older girls' favorite singer, dancer, and actress. Two-year-old Chloe called him Uncle Jell-O after her favorite wiggly snack.

Jaime looked into the solemn brown eyes that held more sorrow than any eight-year-old should ever know.

"You are a part of him, Margeaux. You and your sisters own his heart and soul. When he looks at you, he sees his one dimple on your face. He sees his eyes in Julianna's face, and his hair atop Chloe's head and yours, too.

"But most of all, Margeaux, your daddy loves you and your sisters simply because you exist. That's why he listens to you and plays with you. That's why he makes you do your homework, follow safety rules, eat your vegetables, and say your prayers.

"Your daddy loves you and Julianna and Chloe, Margeaux. Accept that truth as an act of faith supported by how he looks at you, and talks to you, and treats you. That's how you can really tell when someone loves you."

CHAPTER 21

Present Day:

As much as Margeaux sympathized with Theresa and Roderick Cole's plight, she would not collude with them to deceive their only offspring.

"No, Mr. and Mrs. Cole, that's not how the companion services at the LuxeLinks Club work. Full disclosure to all parties and full consent from the member, the companion, and from me is how we conduct business. You may purchase the LuxeLinks Club membership as a gift for your daughter, but Albany is the only person who can negotiate the specific terms of her membership."

Margeaux disliked being the cause of the sudden pall of frustrated disappointment cast upon the older couple's demeanor. Their obvious mutual affection reminded her of the Obamas every time she met with them.

"You've told me that Albany avoids social events. What about mentoring programs? LuxeLinks sponsors professional engagement days where teen girls follow successful women at work for a day or week or month depending on the time of year."

The couple shared a long, silent exchange, then Mrs. Johnson-Cole said, "Our daughter hides behind her camera unless someone expresses genuine interest in photography. That always cures her crippling shyness—at least temporarily."

Margeaux nodded slowly as possibilities swirled in her thoughts. After nearly a minute, she said, "I have an idea."

☙❧

"No! Absolutely not, Margeaux, and don't think giving me that hanging-judge look will change my mind."

Marcus Brandon Thomas, former golf phenom, playboy, and platinum standard for brand endorsements, subsided into the wheeled desk chair behind the work station in the home office of his two-story penthouse with panoramic views he could no longer see of Central Park.

"How can you even tell that I'm giving you a look, Marc?" she asked in the impatient tone he'd become very familiar with during more than a decade of friendship.

"You always huff then slap your palms against your

thighs when you're out of patience with me, and the steady switch from darker to dark in front of my desk tells me that you're pacing. Also, Cedric's tags jingle when he turns his head to keep you in sight.

"Good boy," Marc said when his service animal chuffed in response to hearing his name. "The faint ebb and flow of air, and light whiffs of a floral scent must be from your shampoo or lotion because it's not strong enough for perfume. You're wearing polished cotton trousers with pants legs loose enough to swish softly as you glide across the floor in flat shoes with leather soles."

He heard Margeaux flop into one of the three tufted leather club chairs in front of his desk. "Show off."

The grudging affection in her voice made him laugh. "I've been impressing people with my stunts since I was five years old."

Margeaux's huffy inhalation warned him. "Marc, you worked hard for years to hone your natural affinity for all things golf into being ranked among the top ten golfers in the world every year of your professional career. That isn't a stunt. It's an impressive achievement, sweetheart."

Deep inside his heart and soul, Marc cherished the term of endearment and the tenderness in her voice.

"Save the lovey-dovey stuff for Agent Hard Ass, kiddo," he said. "I know my blindness and my burn scars will not protect me from his wrath if he thinks I'm making the moves on his lady."

Margeaux's lighthearted laugh cheered him even more than her mere presence did. "Jon trusts me, even with a sexy retired pro athlete who used to romance the ladies and party as hard as he worked until turning himself into a mysterious recluse." More softly, she said, "It's been five years, Marc. The surgeries, skin grafts, rehab, experimental treatments, and your mom's homemade cocoa butter worked. The scarring on your face and down your neck resembles waxy tattoos of abstract art. Your locks cover your mangled ear. You look like a beautiful, strong man who survived a horrific fire that would have killed two teenagers and an unborn child if you hadn't saved them. What could you have done differently?"

Marc didn't know. He had no memories of being injured. He remembered partying hard during a round robin of dance clubs with his youngest brother Ronald, dance addict and teetotaler, who ended up driving the Porsche because Marc was too buzzed. They got lost. The GPS kept taking them in circles to nowhere familiar until at four in the morning they decided to check into a retro-looking motor lodge with well-lit parking directly in front of each room.

An hour later, blaring alarms, explosive popping sounds, and the pungent smell of smoke jerked him and his brother awake. They'd each collapsed fully dressed across one of the two full-sized beds crammed into the sparsely furnished room. They were out of the room and in the Porsche in under a minute, carefully backing away from the chaos of burning building and scared, confused people when Marc noticed someone at the far side of the structure. A lanky boy was desperately kicking at a door, then ramming it with his slight shoulder and frantically pulling at the doorknob.

Everything afterward was a blur. Jumping out of the car. Running to the boy. Understanding *my sister* and *pregnant* from the babble of his young voice. Telling Ronald to hold the boy back while Marc backed up to make a running leap to kick the reinforced strike plate. The flimsy wooden door splintered instead. Thick, pungent smoke burned his eyes as he forced his body through the shattered panel. Closing his eyes hadn't stopped them from welling with stinging tears as he croaked, "Steffie," the name he'd heard the boy shout over and over.

When he found her unconscious and fully clothed in the bathtub, the investigators later told him what the many amateur videos confirmed: It was the final explosion of crates of bootleg fireworks that blew a hole in the outer wall and propelled Marcus and the young girl into the air before they landed in the grass behind the motel.

Marc had cocooned the petite teen in his much larger, stronger body, completely protecting her from the impact of the fall and from being coated with the spray of chemicals from the meth lab side business that the illegal fireworks dealers were running out of the room next to the young siblings' hideaway. They had been living there in exchange for their off-the-books maid and building maintenance labors after school and on weekends.

Now, Steffie, her four-year-old daughter, Madeline, and Steffie's older brother, Tyler, all lived with Marc's parents, but on the night of the explosive fire Marc's youngest brother Ronald had used guilt on the teens, and his brother's celebrity on everyone else to get the scared young people placed with a foster family in Queens on the same street with Tanisha and Brandon Thomas to make it easier to keep track of them after they were released from the hospital.

During months of hospitalization, corrective surgeries, physical rehab, bonding with Cedric, learning Braille code, and adjusting to life as a legally blind man, Marcus had relived those few, pivotal minutes of his life countless times. The nearest fire truck had been delayed by a traffic pile-up. Marc was unconscious by the time the second and third trucks and the first ambulance had arrived.

He shook his head toward the spot in front of his desk where a fuzzy Margeaux-shaped silhouette with a vague nimbus of curls blocked the sunshine. He thought about how much his mom and dad were enjoying finally having two girls and another boy to nurture, to guide, to launch into adulthood while providing a safe, loving environment for children that the child welfare system had utterly failed.

"No," he said. "There's nothing I could have done

differently to make sure we all survived that night, Margeaux, but this spontaneous flashback therapy session will not coerce me into attending this event in order to fall in with your latest matchmaking ploy."

Despite her parents' tragic relationship, his friend was a hopeful romantic. He'd realized years ago that she was doing her best to encourage her LuxeLinks Club members and their assigned companions to become friends with the potential for something more. She was always persistent and driven in the pursuit of her goals. Like now.

"Come on, Marc, it's night golf. The balls glow in the dark, and the course is outlined in lights. Every visually impaired player is matched with a sighted partner. I know you still train for hours every day, except Sunday. It's a fundraising event to send poor kids to summer camp. Ten thousand dollars buy-in per player—fun money for you, sweetheart. Come on, Marc, you'll help children who need it and ease the minds of two parents who are worried about their painfully shy, very talented photographer daughter. They don't want her to end up alone after they're dead, which is kind of morbid of them and shouldn't happen for decades, but the mom's an engineer, and the dad's a venture capitalist, so they like to plan for all contingencies."

Exasperated determination underscored her cajoling tone of voice. Marc surrendered to the irresistible force of nature that he'd known as Margeaux Carr Hirsch on a mission since their hasty introduction at a raucous frat party when they were college sophomores making their escape through a delivery entrance at the back of the house, while the police were charging in the front door.

"Only for you would I agree to being a sideshow curiosity while playing a par three course on an ambush date with an unsuspecting photog. How are you and her parents getting her to participate, Margeaux?"

"Her parents already paid for two of the limited spots to play against Big Joe Huntsman's group. They're going to tell Albany they've got a scheduling conflict and need her to go as a representative of their family foundation. It supports accelerated STEM education in underserved public schools."

Marcus's brain chugged. "A photographer named Albany who's the only child of an engineer and a venture capitalist with a family foundation that promotes STEM education—You're setting me up on a blind date with A.M. Cole?"

"Yes."

Marcus slumped against his chair back. "Will donating a million dollars to Big Joe's charity get me out of going to this thing, Margeaux?"

"Nope, reclusive golf snob. It's past time for you to emerge from this luxurious cave for more than early morning, afternoon, and evening walks with your loyal household staff. They're worried about you."

Yeah. Marcus was going to have a little chat with

those loving blabbermouths. "You owe me big time for this, Margeaux, and I plan to collect."

"Oh, good!" she said, the volume of her satisfaction obscuring the sounds of rustling fabric, the movement of stiff canvas, and shuffling papers before a few stacked pages nudged one of his hands flat against his desktop. "Here are all the details, Marc."

He closed his eyes.

He usually reminded himself to keep his eyes closed because the gift of being able to see bright lights and shadows, which gave him some depth perception, also gave him excruciating headaches from eye strain.

At this moment, he used the act of concentrating on smoothing his fingertips over the neatly arranged dots of Braille code to hide his unexpected surge of emotion.

Marcus had made his peace with being legally blind years ago, Margeaux was his only friend who had integrated communications software and hardware designed to meet the needs of the blind into her daily routine as soon as he'd told her that his significant vision loss was permanent. She'd done it months before anyone else in his life had, including his parents and siblings.

Margeaux was his forever friend. One night of golf with a photographer whose controversial Ugly Subjects travelling exhibit drew praise and protests for its aggressive depictions of marginalized people and their physical scars was a small price to pay as a gesture of appreciation for all that Margeaux's friendship added to his life.

He and Albany Cole would get along just fine as long as she kept her camera shuttered around him.

CHAPTER 22

Suckered by her well-intentioned, control freak, matchmaking parents again, Albany thought with self-deprecating good humor as she stood next to Marcus Brandon Thomas while staffers kitted them out with two sets of glow-in-the-dark golf clubs, balls, tees, and everything else they loaded into the cart before other staff members checked the fit of their reflective safety vests. Cedric's service animal harness and vest exceeded the visibility requirement.

"Nine holes. Two balls per foursome. Bragging rights to the team with the lowest score and the team with the fastest time. Merciless ridicule to the teams who are worst and slowest," Big Joe Huntsman said, then reminded them of the rules of play. Using cell phones or sports cams would disqualify an entire group, in addition to incurring a five-thousand-dollar penalty, as stated in the contract under the terms of participation.

As the host of the event, his group was teeing off first, but once Joe had recognized the former golf phenom during his warm-up in a secluded practice area, he'd drafted Marcus as an impromptu co-host to tee off first with Albany and two pharmaceutical company CEOs who alternated between gushing like golf geek fanboys and silently staring at Marcus like hypnotized subjects waiting for a signal from their golf idol.

Obviously, Big Joe was savvy enough to improvise on the fly because the first public sighting of Marcus Brandon Thomas on a golf course five years after his heroic actions saved three lives and ended his storied career, when he was on the cusp of achieving legendary status, would generate media buzz across all platforms and categories.

Getting Marcus to open the round was a show of opportunistic marketing genius.

Albany leaned closer to speak into his undamaged ear. "Hope your innate golf mojo has a proximity component, Marcus, because although I've golfed many times before, I'm a total klutz without a camera in my hands, and the other two golfers in our quartet look like they're going to pass out from the excitement of golfing with you."

∽∾∽

Her wry tone made him smile. Their earlier perfunctory introduction hadn't revealed the full range of the husky grit of her soft voice.

"You're sure it's not horrified silence from seeing my injuries up close?" he whispered.

In the incomplete silence, Marcus let the ambient sounds of moving carts, jostling clubs, shuffling feet, and bodies walking away from him farther into the rough inform his perception about what was happening around him, on the course, while he waited for her answer. He felt the weight of her focused regard sweep over his face as he stroked the collapsible cane hooked by a carbiner in its usual place on one of the belt loops over his back pocket.

Touching his face every day for the past five years always confirmed what his family, doctors, and staff told him about his appearance in subtle and direct, unintended and deliberate ways. At the first removal of the bandages, he had looked monstrous. His mom's weeping, Dad's harsh in-drawn breath, along with the doctor's calm assurances about the high success rates of modern reconstructive surgery had clued him into the fact that the tight pull of skin from the mangled remains of the shell of his ear to the outer corner of his left eye to the mid-point of that cheekbone, over his jaw, down the side of his neck, shoulder cap, shoulder blade, ribcage and hip all the way to his ankle looked as horrible as his body felt.

Now, that same swath of skin felt like a relatively

supple waxy smooth length of flesh mismatched with the rest of his undamaged skin, making him a human patchwork.

"You look like a privileged man who was strong enough to survive a horrific fire, Marcus Brandon Thomas. You look like all the reasons why young golfers still wear your edgy, urban MBT brand of clothing and use your equipment. You look healed and vigilant and ready, like an ethical man who has a prestigious annual award for extraordinary acts of courage named for him by the Endowment of Pro-Am Golfers."

Moved by her unexpected words, Marcus said, "Thank you, Albany. Let's go play."

ങ

As Marcus stood holding a club while preparing to tee off on an actual golf course for the first time in five years, he pushed aside thoughts about the differences between private daily indoor training with customized weighted clubs with only Cedric as his furry sentinel, and outdoor play in front of a captive audience of strangers.

Eyes closed, he filled his lungs with a deep inhale, then touched the tip of his tongue to the roof of his mouth and breathed out through his slightly parted lips as he relaxed his shoulders and swiveled his hips in a movement of loose figure-eights in one direction, then the reverse until he settled his weight into stillness to setup his stance to address the ball.

"He's doing that thing he always does," one of the pharmaceutical execs whispered.

"I know! Shut up!" the other exec hissed.

Their voices registered without disturbing his concentration. In his mind's eye, the bright lights outlining the boundaries of the course, the sand traps, hazards, pins, and flags nudged his memories of playing here as a sighted child. He let those memories underscore the current sensory input before he adjusted his grip and prepared to coil into his swing.

✍✍✍

Albany wished her camera were in her hands and not locked away in the trunk of her car because Marcus Brandon Thomas was magnificent.

The motion of his powerful, muscular height looked like classical statuary in motion as he rotated into the arc of his beautiful swing, launching the glowing ball in a low streak through the night sky to land within yards of the first hole. The service animal's reflective vest shimmied with what appeared to be Cedric's thwarted desire to give chase.

The sudden applause was deafening.

✍✍✍

Blind luck or muscle memory ingrained after thousands of hours of study, training, inversion therapy, and practice, and more than two decades of competitive play and dissection of every aspect of his and every other master golfer's game, Marcus wondered as he released his hold on the club when Albany said, "It was almost a hole in one." And someone else said, "I'll take that for you, sir," before a slight tug pulled it from his hand.

"Thank you."

"My pleasure, sir."

Marcus recognized the awe in the caddy's young voice as a soft hand clasped his at the same time that Cedric guided him to step aside to make room for the next golfer in his foursome.

"Adjust your alignment," Marcus said to one of the drug execs.

"Huh?" It was the bombastic whisperer.

"Your labored breathing tells me that you're excited, but also that your torso is out of alignment."

A soft murmur from the gallery of participants burbled around them.

"Level chin. Ears over your relaxed, rolled back shoulders over hips over ankles opens up your diaphragm and engages your core, which aligns your torso and eases your breathing to allow you to draw from the strength of your entire body start to finish through your swing. Try it, then step out to set your heels wider than your shoulders and softly flex your knees. Visualize your weight shift and rotation as one integrated action."

Albany marveled at the calm patience with which Marcus instructed geeky golf fanboy number one. Marcus's sedate tone and easy stance were in stark contrast to his crushing grip on her left hand with his right while this charity night golfing event morphed into a basic skills clinic.

"May I demonstrate with you, Albany?" Marcus asked her at the second hole, where one of the hardcore flirts kept insisting that she didn't understand what he meant by meeting the ball just before the bottom of the arc in her swing.

Albany imagined being held against all of the physical power of Marcus's lean, muscular height and breadth as his slanted smile brushed her ear while the deep register of his voice told her what to do. "Yes," she said.

To the very pretty flirt, Marcus said, "Watch first, then practice what you see," before his fragrant warmth blanketed Albany's back, butt, and thighs.

He suggested that anyone who was serious about their golf game should keep a journal to record their strokes and performance to assess their development. Practice in front of a mirror and record themselves on video if possible. He also suggested that studying human anatomy was helpful.

His arms came around her body, and his hands hovered over her grip on the club.

"I'm going to talk you through each step of establishing the angle of my spine and locating the bottom of my arc. Please mirror each of my moves, Albany."

"All right," she said, relaxing into the warm curve of his strong body. He smelled like night blooming plants and freshly turned, baked earth.

∽∾∽

As Albany's lush curves molded themselves into the front of his body from shoulders to feet, Marcus recognized his tactical miscalculation a half-beat after his body responded to their physical contact.

He didn't need to see Albany to know that she was beautiful. He could hear it in her voice and in the interest in the other men's voices when they spoke to her. The competitive edge in the persistent flirt's tone told Marcus that the woman viewed Albany as her only serious rival for his attention.

With Albany in his arms, Marcus allowed himself a few seconds to enjoy the soft caress of her fluffy curls against his chin as they stood up straight. Scent memories of the Caribbean filled his lungs when he inhaled. She didn't shift her magnificent ass away from the prod of his dick. She pressed closer, which sparked fantasies of being naked in this same position with her and inside her, holding her in place to feel the slap of his crotch against the two supple rounds of flesh while he drove them both into hard, fast orgasm.

In addition to the sexual, her body, her scent, her voice called to his long dormant emotional hunger for the kind of smart, generous, unflappable, funny woman Albany seemed to be.

Marcus pushed out his distracting thoughts with his full-lung exhalation then stood up straight before bending at the waist, cueing Albany and his unseen observers to each move as he executed it, and her limbs flowed into alignment with his as if they were repeating a familiar tandem routine.

CHAPTER 23

Albany suspended all of her conscious brain functions outside of sinking her body into his, to use Marcus like her own personal human exoskeleton, and listening to the confident command of his deep voice as he explained each move and its purpose.

Albany imagined hearing his voice say, "Bend over at the waist and flex your knees. We're going to fuck hard and fast until we both come enough to take off the edge, then we're going to make love."

As their arms swung up and their upper bodies rotated in tandem, Albany worked not to experience a screaming orgasm while being held in the arms of a man she'd just met and standing in front of two dozen strangers.

Only seven more holes to endure.

෬෩෬

"Did you let me win, Marc?" Big Joe sounded dead serious as he leaned in during their handshake at four a.m. according to his internal clock and chiming watch with a voice feature.

Marcus laughed. "I sincerely thank you for the compliment, Joe, if you believe that my rusty golf skills are good enough after five years and blindness for me to manipulate the outcome of this round."

Marcus reached out and smiled when Albany's soft palm met his. He linked their fingers and tugged her closer to his side.

"Is there a back way out of here, Joe? We want to avoid socializing at the breakfast melee in the clubhouse."

Albany didn't refute his presumptuous inclusion of her in his request, which confirmed his suspicions about Albany's forceful style of play as a symptom of her shyness and as an attempt to muscle through her obligation to participate as quickly as possible.

Joe said, "Sure," before thanking Albany and expressing his warm regards to her parents as he led them away from the adrenaline-hyped golfers who had accepted Marc's cordial congratulations and farewells as the polite dismissals they were.

The jumble of their excited voices rose and fell on sharing their favorite tips and strokes and shots and strategy philosophies shared with them by the great golfer most of them now admired even more.

The flat grade and smooth pavement made it easy for

Marcus to match Joe's pace as he led them to the parking lot where his car and driver waited for him.

"Your driver's pulling up right now, Marc," Joe said. "I've got to get back to glad-hand and supervise the others while we all relive our glorious golf encounter with you, but may I call you next week? There's a business proposition I'd like you to consider."

"Sure." Marcus offered his cell phone to Joe so the other man could enter their numbers into each phone.

"Thanks for coming tonight, Marc. You just made our inaugural fundraising event for the Huntsman Camps Four Kids Foundation more successful than I'd imagined. Talk to you in a few days.

"Goodnight or, rather, good morning, Albany. Drive safely."

More farewells were exchanged among them until Joe left them and Marcus introduced Albany to his full-time driver, Osgood, who cheerfully acknowledged her before he asked Marcus if they were escorting the young lady to her home.

"Oh, no, thank you, but I drove," she said. "My car is just over there." Her gesture raised their linked hands to the left for a few seconds. Albany leaned closer to whisper into Marcus's undamaged ear. "Mercy duty completed, golf ace. Whatever bribe my parents offered you, I hope you made them pay up front. Otherwise, they'll try to squeeze you into another event. They're very tricky about things like that."

Because Marcus heard exasperated affection underscored by humorous resignation in her voice, he told her the truth. "Actually, I'm the one who paid to be here with you tonight, Albany."

Two heavy taps of shoes against asphalt, the opening snick of a car door, then the gentle slamming of it closed told Marcus that Osgood had removed himself as a witness, giving him nothing to report when Mrs. Osgood and Marc's family tried to grill him later.

ᴄᴈᴇᴈ

"Oh, dear lord, don't tell me they've added extortion to their underhanded matchmaking toolbox of schemes. Their victims usually at least benefit from their sacrifices by getting something like sky box passes or generous donations to their charitable foundations."

Albany was mortified, but the fact that Marcus was still tightly holding her hand while he stood next to her with a broad tilted grin on his face encouraged her, even though the downward pull at the left corner of his mouth gave the impression of a doubtful smirk.

"What leverage did my parents use against you?"

He shook his head as his smile turned rueful. "Not them—my friend, Margeaux Hirsch, decided my re-entry into society was overdue. And that this event offered the double benefit of forcing me out of my cave while giving your parents what they wanted for you."

Albany groaned. "Of course, my parents sought help from The Feminist Madam Matchmaker of the Rich and Powerful." She could tell from Marcus's abrupt burst of laughter that he was as amused by the title of his friend's unauthorized biography as Albany was. "They probably tried to buy me a LuxeLinks Club membership and select their idea of a perfect companion for me."

His diplomatic silence confirmed her educated guess.

"Well, Marcus, you looked like you were enjoying yourself, and everyone else loved watching a master in action and learning from you, so I'll shake off my proxy guilt over my parents' behavior."

Albany relaxed her fingers in his loose grip.

"Thank you for making what I'd expected to be an awkward ordeal into an enjoyable occasion," she said as her thoughts floundered for a diplomatic escape phrase.

"Will you come to my home for breakfast, Albany?"

His fingers tightened painlessly on hers when she started to release his hand.

"You've already gone above and beyond, Marcus. No need to feed me, too."

He gently tugged her a little closer to his side. "I'm starving, Albany. Please don't make me eat alone. Cedric likes it when I miss my mouth, but he's a terrible conversationalist, which is why he flunked part of his service animal final exam. For eating table scraps, not for being a bad conversationalist. Say yes, Albany. You can follow us into the city and park in my building's underground garage."

Other than gently squeezing her hand and tugging her a little closer, Marcus did nothing to convince her to agree. He simply stood and waited. At his feet, Cedric sat and waited, too.

The dog was back in his reflective vest and harness, which Marcus had removed after the first hole to indicate off-duty status so his furry helper would feel released to nap in a cozy corner on the back of their assigned golf cart until the end of the event.

Man and beast exuded irresistible appeal.

"Yes."

She entered his address into her phone as a backup, even though Marcus promised her that his driver would make it easy for her to follow them.

⌘

Marcus was excited, and nervous to have a woman who wasn't his long-time friend or relative or employee in his home for the first time in the five years since the accident that had taken his sight, his career, and a crippling chunk of his identity.

Albany had grabbed his hand as soon as they'd stepped out of the elevator and into the lobby. Its security and sophistication had sold him on living here even before he'd seen the views from the renovated penthouse apartment.

After being greeted by the reception staff, Marcus, Albany, Osgood and even Cedric remained silent inside the completely restored, original Art Deco express elevator retrofitted with modern technology. Being hit with the scents of bacon, bread, and roasted vegetables when the elevator doors opened onto his private lobby told him that his housekeeper had defied his personal security manager again by leaving the door to the penthouse open in anticipation of his arrival.

Mrs. Osgood saw herself as the boss of all of them, Marcus included.

His security guy had likely decided to avoid starting his day with another losing battle with the house manager.

"Welcome to my home, Albany."

ೞഏೞഏ

She was impressed, which was noteworthy because she had been raised on her parents' Westchester estate once owned by a Woolworth heir. And their extended family and friends and business associates lived in similar levels of luxury, but it was the hominess against the backdrop of panoramic views of the sunrise over Central Park in the two-story apartment that most impressed her.

Throughout Marcus's introductions to his house manager, his chef, and his bodyguard to her, Albany scolded herself to focus on the people she was meeting, not sunshine-filled open spaces, glossy hardwood floors, and simple arrangements of big, soft furniture oriented toward the windows framing spectacular plein air views of the heart of New York City.

"Yes, Mrs. Osgood, breakfast in the greenhouse sounds perfect."

When his staff departed, Marcus knelt to remove Cedric's harness and reflective vest.

"Being physically unrestrained releases him from active duty," Marcus said as he stood. "But Cedric will follow me everywhere anyway if I'm alone, even if I command him to stay or lie down. That's another reason why he landed on the list of hardship service animal placements."

The dog bumped Albany's hand until she started petting him, which jingled his tags and whipped his wagging tail into high gear while she cooed praises to him for being a smart, pretty boy.

Albany and Marcus both laughed when Cedric barked in agreement.

"Now you've done it, Albany. Furry chaperone guaranteed. He's a glutton for affection and praise."

With Cedric at his side, Marcus linked the fingers of his right hand with her left hand before he confidently led her across the wide area of the living room, billiards table, and indoor putting green leading out to the wraparound terrace.

From the outside, the greenhouse tucked in the corner resembled a giant topiary with a hidden door under a leafy gable.

Albany gasped with delighted surprise.

"It's constructed from climbing evergreen vines, evergreen trees, and potted bamboo lattices," he said as they stepped inside the cool, dim interior. The smell of sun-baked foliage and loamy soil was pleasing in its richness.

"The HOA board unanimously approved it after the consulting horticulturist showed them pictures from my junior pro golf tour of the Chichibu prefecture in Japan years ago." He paused, the sighed. "How many candles, Albany?"

She laughed as he reached forward until his free hand collided with a chair back. She waited until they were both seated with Cedric lying down in the space between their two chairs before she answered.

"A simple arrangement of three fat dandelion yellow candles on a hammered gold tray in the center of four covered dishes and a basket of thick, toasted bread quarters. White table cloth. Green and gray houndstooth napkins. Everything's charming, Marcus.

"May I serve you some of each dish?" she asked as she pulled up the hinged lids on one chafing dish at a time until both of their plates were full.

Between bites of succulent fare and sips of what tasted like a freshly squeezed blend of grapefruit, apple, orange and carrot juice, and the occasional score for Cedric whenever Marcus suspiciously miscalculated the distance from his plate to his mouth, breakfast lasted for more than two hours filled with funny recaps of the drug execs' top ten geeky golf fanboy moments and serious confessions from Marcus about how good and terrified he'd felt walking the links again.

He asked Albany about her travels and photography subjects and her next project.

"Powerful Subjects from maids to truckers, stay-at-home parents, and heads of state. My first shoot is at the LuxeLinks Beach Club with the CEO of HelioSun Tech Hub during her vacation this August." Saying the month got elongated on a huge yawn.

CHAPTER 24

Cedric popped up unto all fours when Marcus pushed back from the table.

"Okay, Albany, of course, you're excused, but that's your third yawn. Let's get you settled into a guestroom for some shut-eye, or I can have Osgood drive you home in your car, then he can catch the train back."

Marcus didn't let offering her options keep him from smoothly herding their little group back inside all the way to the foot of the engineering genius of the cantilevered staircase. Albany reached out to touch the textured edge of one of the higher treads. "Why are the edges rough?"

"My very own rumble strips to warn me. They also glow in the dark for the same reason."

Butting his head gently into Marcus's thigh, Cedric barked.

"Later for the twenty-dollar tour, Albany, since my impatient furry chaperone is tired and wants us to head upstairs. Bossiness also flunked him out of being an unconditionally certified service animal." Marcus extended his hand toward her with uncanny accuracy. "Shall we?"

Albany linked her fingers with his before she followed man and dog up the securely anchored, floating staircase.

෨෧෨

Marcus chose to escort Albany into the first bedroom at the top of the staircase because he needed to keep her as far away from his master suite as possible for the sake of his revved body, peace of mind, and honorable intentions. Consecutive hours of breathing in the subtle layers of her fragrant scent and listening to the alto range of her soft voice while holding her delicate hand or being wrapped around her supple body, when she'd graciously agreed to act as his test pupil during the night golf event, all tested the limits of his self-control.

Right now Albany smelled like all of his favorite things rolled into one: woman, sunshine, grass, the pure sweat of exertion on the links.

He wanted to kiss her. He craved another hug from her—one that was longer and more intimate than the spontaneous one she'd initiated in celebration of their group's second place finish. Being in her arms had reactivated his desire for contact with a woman who wasn't a relative, platonic friend, employee or business associate.

Almost a year ago was the last time he'd paid for a professional vetted by Osgood to meet Marcus in a barely lit room at a generic chain hotel to satisfy him with her mouth. His hand offered greater emotional connection.

He wanted to kiss Albany and continue kissing her until the kissing expanded into other pleasures.

୧୨୧୨

Leaving Marcus and Cedric hovering in the doorway, Albany dropped her handbag on a low baroque console table and stepped farther into the uncluttered elegance of the luxurious sunny room that still exuded warm welcome in its complimentary color scheme, textures, and shapes.

"The attached bath is through the closet. Mrs. Osgood keeps it stocked with towels and a variety of bath stuff," Marcus said.

"Thank you," Albany said while the man's white undershirt, navy blue gym shorts, pin-striped dress shirt, and full-length terry cloth robe laid out across the turned back duvet caught her attention.

"I think she also raided your wardrobe to give me a variety of sleepwear. Please thank her for me."

୧୨୧୨

"I will," Marcus said. He thought he would definitely express his gratitude to Mrs. Osgood for her decision to loan Albany some of his clothes, rather than her own, even though his house manager was similar in height and size to his unexpected guest.

He liked imagining Albany wearing his clothes against her soft skin while she slept in his home.

After he told her about the laundry chute in the bathroom, Marcus asked, "Do you want to wake up at a certain time?"

"I'll set the alarm on my phone for two o'clock this afternoon, unless you need me gone earlier, Marcus."

Her voice came closer to him with every short, faint slide of her socks against hardwood. He felt the warmth of her proximity before she whispered, "Thank you for taking such good care of me on the golf course and afterward."

Her soft lips brushed his then paused. Waiting.

⌘⌘

Initiating the kiss hadn't been much of a risk for Albany since Marcus's implacable grip on her hand throughout the night whenever he hadn't been golfing or wrapped around her body had provided solid physical evidence that he was sexually attracted to her.

He hadn't encouraged any of the other women who'd flirted with him, which suggested that his attraction was specific to Albany, not just random convenience.

When the sudden clasp of his big, strong hands at her waist lifted her to the tips of her socked toes and Marcus tilted his head to transform their kiss from chaste contact to in-depth sensory engagement, Albany silently cheered her own audacity as she reached up to ensnare some of the soft round strands of his beautifully groomed, smoothly rolled shoulder-length locks that had come free of the black metal clip at the base of his neck.

❧❦❧

Marcus thought that grabbing Albany and adding more heat to their kiss must have tripped her internal switch from idle to overdrive because she was suddenly all over him: eating at his mouth, pulling his hair, jerking his hair clip until it loosened and clinked to the floor—all while climbing his body and not stopping until her legs were around his waist, and he was leaning against the wall just inside the room to support the weight of both of their bodies.

Beneath the sounds of panting breath, fabric friction, skin slide, and smacking, suckling kisses, Marcus heard an indignant chuff before the soft jingle of Cedric's tags headed away from the guestroom and toward his master suite at the end of the hall.

Sliding his two-handed grip from Albany's waist to her magnificent ass, Marcus shuffled forward twenty-one and a half paces to the near side of the guest bed, turned, and dropped backward.

He got into a comfortable rhythm of squeezing, stroking, and fondling her butt while Albany ravished his mouth, pulled his hair, and frantically worked her crotch over his hard dick in the hottest session of dry humping he had ever experienced.

❡❡❡

Albany was so close to coming so hard. His spread fingers dug into the divide of her buttocks, and the heels of his hands pressed, controlling the angle and speed of her undulating hips grinding her vulva over his groin.

The effusive wetness of her response caused the cotton crotch of her panties to move across her clitoris and labia in a sticky slide that saturated the seam of her pastel yellow pants.

She moaned into his mouth when her urgent attempts to fight his hold succeeded only in frustrating her more. She lifted her mouth from his.

Once Albany could speak coherently, she said, "Marcus, please tell me that Mrs. Osgood stocks your bathrooms with condoms."

"Mrs. Osgood always stocks all of the bathrooms with condoms." He sing-songed the words around his lopsided smile.

Albany didn't let his grunting laugh slow her leap

from atop his body to the floor, across the distance to the closet, down its short aisle leading to the bath, where she found a variety pack of enough premium condoms to supply an orgy.

"I hope you pay Mrs. Osgood very generously," Albany said after she returned to the bedroom and resumed her perch atop Marcus.

"Generously enough for her and her husband to resist temptation every time one of my visitors tries to lure…Ah—" His words stopped when she unbuckled his belt, unbuttoned and unzipped his fly, and pulled his erection free of his boxer briefs.

She wrapped the fingers of one of her hands tightly around his length and squeezed, pumping him a few times before she rolled the condom over him. His pounding fists against the mattress punctuated his guttural moan.

"Hurry," he said with a depth of demanding supplication that had her unbuckling and unfastening her own belt and pants in seconds.

She shimmied and wiggled and kicked free of fabric until she was bare from her waist to her ankles and able to mount him as she swung her legs astride his crotch and sank low.

The depth and stretch of accommodating the length and breadth of him held her senses suspended at the farthest edge of pleasure.

જાજ

Reaching up with both hands, Marcus said, "Come here, Albany."

Her slow descent tormented his dick with the second by second changes in the angle of her juicy cunt's squeezing grip. He stripped her out of her waffle-weave golf shirt, leaving her dressed only in a smooth bra that felt like the practical sports variety to his fingertips. He shoved it up and wrestled it off of her before he pulled her down to his chest and wrapped her in his arms while Albany's lips mapped the damaged side of his face and neck with kisses. He could feel the soft ends of her hair trailing the curve of her cheek, the line of her chin, and the brush of her nose.

The surface of her warm, smooth skin acted like a magnet to the palms of his hands, which Marcus couldn't resist stroking his fingertips down the nape of her neck to the delicate line of her shoulders and the subtle relief of her shoulder blades. He gently tapped out a count of her vertebrae and explored the indentations of the two small dimples at the base of her spine before he grabbed her ass again and squeezed, using his hold to rock her hips and rub her clitoris against his groin, the only part of his body that was exposed below his neck.

A full-body caress of his naked skin to her naked skin posed too much risk for rejection if Albany's eyes could see the marred skin hidden by his long-sleeved shirt and pants. The way she was kissing the damaged skin down the side of his face and neck was a good sign, but he wasn't willing to risk abruptly ending what he hoped was only the first of many intimate moments with this fascinating woman by showing her all of his scars.

Marcus planned to pleasure Albany into a sexual stupor that would addict her to his touch and trump her revulsion once she was exposed to the consequences of his physical injuries.

⁓⁓⁓

Being full between her legs while the hard strength of his hands squeezed her butt and rocked her whole body against the woven performance material of his shirt and pants abraded her skin and drugged her senses with the decadent contrasts of being on top of Marcus and riding his fully clothed body while she wore only white cotton footies with rainbow pom-poms at the back of her ankles.

The steady rocking motion rubbed her nipples back and forth over the developed muscularity of his chest, but Albany kept her hands cupped around his head to keep his mouth under hers as her body exploded into orgasm.

She bore down on his erection with her hips and her vaginal muscles until accepting the unbearable pleasure lifted her mouth from his on a gasp, that turned into a scream, as she took him deeper with each rocking thrust.

⁓⁓⁓

Marcus held off his orgasm until Albany collapsed

into a sweaty, loose-limbed heap atop his body. He rolled, getting her flat on her back under him, going to his knees, lifting her ankles to his shoulders, and claiming her with deep, hard strokes in and out of the clingy wetness of her cunt.

He made it last for as long as he could, then he let go.

ೋೋೋ

"Are you and Uncle Mark-Us taking a nap?" a sweet, high-pitched voice whispered to Albany. Very loudly.

The strong arm around her waist pulled her closer to the muscular warmth blanketing her back, but Marcus's breathing stayed in the steady respiration of deep sleep while Albany opened her heavy eyelids to stare into the curious gaze of a dark-eyed, brown-skinned pixie with thin Kente cloth ribbons decorating her two afro puffs. The little girl's dimples showed when she smiled.

"Maddy!" an exasperated feminine voice called from somewhere on the staircase.

That woke Marcus instantly, stripping the duvet and sheets from their bodies to drop to their waists when he popped up into sitting on the mattress. He moved his head around from side to side in sleepy confusion.

"What?"

Albany gave silent thanks for the fact that Marcus was decently covered in his shirt and boxer briefs while she was wearing only his undershirt, which she didn't remember putting on. At least it covered her to mid-thigh.

"Maddy!" said much closer and with more exasperation this time as the little girl who was dressed in a pinkT-shirt with Thor on the front, red denim shorts, and tiny red leather boat shoes kicked off her shoes, then scrambled up into the bed and squirmed her way into the space between Albany and Marcus.

"Grandma! I waked up Uncle Marc and his lady friend!"

"Madeline Marcia Thomas, you know better than to barge into someone's room."

"But the door was open, Grandma, and Uncle Marc and his lady friend didn't say nothing when I knocked."

"They didn't say anything, Maddy."

The little girl shook her head.

"No, Grandma, they didn't."

Albany smiled at Maddy's grandma, who shook her head with enough force to sway the ends of her long, silvery gray Sisterlocks against the V-neck of her colorful paisley-patterned maxi dress. The woman resembled a feminine, unscarred, more seasoned version of Marcus.

"Hello, Mrs. Thomas, I'm—"

"Albany Cole a.k.a. A.M. Cole, who uses photography as social commentary about Ugly Subjects. There's quite a bit of online speculation about you and my oldest son today." Her laser-sharp gaze swung away from Albany's eyes to pin her granddaughter in place as the little girl started scooting under the sheets.

"Come back downstairs with Grandma, Maddy, so your uncle and his friend can get ready to come downstairs for dinner."

The little girl jumped to her feet on top of the bed linens. "Okay, Grandma," she said before she smacked a kiss on her uncle's jaw then turned and did the same to Albany's cheek. "Hurry up, please, I'm hungry!"

Maddy hopped over Albany's legs, dropped to her stomach, then held onto the edge of the duvet as she scooted backward and lowered herself over the edge of the bed like an experienced free climber to sit on the floor to put her shoes back on her small feet.

Her head and shoulders briefly disappeared under the bed, where a muffled exchange between girl and dog ended with giggles and a soft bark before Maddy reappeared and jumped up to run over to her grandma.

By the time woman and child were halfway down the staircase, judging from the sounds of their retreat, Marcus still hadn't spoken another word.

Albany slung her arm around his waist and tilted her chin up to kiss his bristled jaw. "A little sluggish on the rise and shine, golf ace?"

His lopsided grin charmed her when he turned his head and leaned down to kiss her. "Had three alarm clocks in college because my mom wasn't there to whack me into consciousness with the whip of her voice," he said, scooping her into his arms as he moved to get out of bed.

"Let's shower in my room. We'll find you some presentable clothes as armor because Maddy is usually the advance scout for family ambushes. I think there's an invasion of Thomases waiting for us downstairs."

He set her on her feet then linked his fingers with hers as Cedric belly-crawled out from under the bed to guide them out of the guestroom and down the hall to the master suite.

If the Thomas family had read about her and Marcus online today, then so had her lovely, overbearing parents. Albany needed to unearth her handbag from wherever she'd dropped it in the bedroom and check her phone, which she'd forgotten all about as soon as Marcus had taken control of their initial kiss.

ღღღ

Clean and dressed in one of Marcus's white linen dress shirts half unbuttoned over one of his tank undershirts with the cuffs rolled neatly up to her elbows, both shirt hems loosely tied just below the waistband of a plain, matte navy blue pair of his running leggings to create a blousy hourglass silhouette that flattered her butt and camouflaged her lack of a bra, Albany was listening to her mom on the phone while watching Marcus shave with short, precise strokes of a shiny silver razor. From his spot seated at her feet, Cedric was back on duty in his vest and harness. He watched his human with rapt vigilance.

"No, Mom…Yes, dinner tomorrow with you and Dad sounds good…No, I'll meet you at the restaurant at eight…Love you, too."

She quickly jabbed her thumb against the display screen.

"That seemed relatively painless once you assured her that you weren't being held against your will," Marcus said in a pause between strokes over his chin after she ended the call with an audible sigh.

"Oh, no, that easy chat is supposed to lull me into a false sense of comfort before tomorrow night's inquisition. Torquemada's got nothing on my parents. Thumb screws are for posers. The unblinking Gaze of Disappointment works every time." She paused to admire the results of his completely bloodless, close shave. "Did someone teach you that?" she asked at the same time Marcus asked, "Do you want me to come as backup?"

He spoke first into the shocked silence as each of them waited for the other to continue.

"My beard won't grow over the damaged skin, so I practiced using a razor for a week without the blade to get comfortable with moving it over my skin without being able to see what I'm doing."

Albany filed away his answer while another part of her brain considered his question about backing her up at dinner with her parents tomorrow night. "Yes, Marcus,

I'd love to have you by my side tomorrow night, but since I'm interested in dating you, I'll spare you."

The thick cotton hand towel he was using to blot his face muffled his laughter. "Let's see if you still want to date me after you meet all of the Thomases who are downstairs."

CHAPTER 25

As they reached the bottom tread, Marcus heard the voices of everyone in his immediate family except for Steffie, Maddy's mom and his legally adopted little sister, who was a full-time college undergrad majoring in biology as a stepping stone to pre-med.

In the silence caused by his entry into the open main living space, Maddy's sweet voice chirped, "See, I told you Albany is nice and pretty. She is too a smart babe just like Papa Brand said Uncle Marc likes."

As he speculated that his only niece could hear in her sleep and listen through walls, Marcus felt a tug on his hand holding Albany's. The angle of the pull suggested that Albany was kneeling, and the quick scuff of Maddy's running steps told him that the collision that was known in the family as an enthusiastic Mad hug was seconds away from impact.

"Umph," Albany breathed as their tethered arms swung from the force of sudden impact.

"Thank you, Maddy. Kind words from smart girls like you are lovely to hear." She used her handholding connection with Marcus to keep her balance as she stood. "Will you introduce me to your family, Maddy?"

⌒⌒⌒

Marcus had not exaggerated when he'd warned her that his entire family was probably downstairs. Tanisha and Brandon Thomas had allowed their granddaughter to introduce them and her very young adult Uncle Tyler before they'd mentioned that Mrs. Osgood wanted Maddy's help in the kitchen, which sent the little dynamo bolting out of the room with a smacking kiss to her blind uncle's free hand and quick waves to Albany and her grandparents.

After a few moments of shared laughter, Albany met the married middle brothers, Turner and Edmund; their lovely wives, Jessamyn and Britte; and their teenage sons. Each couple had two, which clarified earlier remarks Marcus had made during breakfast about Steffie and Maddy as delayed answers to his parents' prayers for a daughter to raise. Four biological sons, one adopted son, and four grandsons equaled a lot of testosterone. Unmarried Ronald constantly teased quiet young Tyler then defended himself by saying, "Hey, that's what Marc, Turner, and Edmund used to do to me, when I was the baby brother. It means I love you in Neanderthal."

Albany could see that Ronald's casual declaration of affection pleased Tyler very much.

Maddy charged back into the room. "Mrs. Goodies says it's time for dinner! Yay!"

Her energetic happy dance involved an intricate combination of hand flapping, head shaking, and wiggling while hopping from one foot to the other.

Her grandpa scooped her up into his arms on his way to the large oval dining table.

⊘⊘⊘

Pandemonium was too tame to describe sitting down to a meal with his family under normal circumstances. Tonight, Albany's presence at his side pushed the limits of their self-restraint.

Their comments and questions were genial and mostly appropriate, but he could tell that they had spent the hours between reading about her involvement with him at the night golf charity event and invading his home with discovering as much about Albany Cole as possible. During his junior tournament years, one of his parents or now-deceased grandparents had always traveled with him. During his long recovery after saving Tyler and a pregnant Steffie, his parents, brothers, and sisters-in-law had all taken shifts of staying with him in the hospital and rehab center and going with him to his out-patient appointments. They tried hard to respect his independence, but all of them were protective of Marcus, even Tyler and Steffie, who felt like they owed him a huge debt no matter how often he told them that their health and happiness, loving their parents, studying and working hard all made losing his sight worth the cost. Maddy was worth more than that fire had taken from him. On his worst days, that truth helped him to choose to keep moving forward.

"So my first-born son participated in a charitable fundraising event at a golf course in Queens but didn't think he should visit his retired mom and dad for breakfast at our home, also in Queens? Didn't want to discuss with his folks how it felt to play golf publicly for the first time in five years."

Marcus knew that his mom's pleasant tone of voice and calm cadence were for Maddy's benefit.

He answered her last question first. "I felt sick to my stomach and like I'd come home after a lifetime of exile." He reached out with his right hand, and Albany's soft palm met his. "When our group placed second, I felt reborn, and I wanted to savor that feeling. And I wanted to spend some private time getting to know Albany Cole, who whispered a visually descriptive running commentary throughout the night. She let me use her as my demonstration pupil and as a shield against persistent flirts and aggressive curiosity seekers. I wanted to be with the woman who treated me like a man she was interested in knowing better. "Okay, Mom?"

After a very loaded pause, she said, "Yes, baby. Okay."

A fork clattered onto a dinner plate.

"That's 'cuz Albany likes smart babies, too!" Maddy declared around a bite of meatball from the garbled sound of her perky voice.

Their shared laughter released all of the remaining tension from the group.

∞

Two hours later, Albany asked, "Everybody in your family hugged and kissed me goodbye as a sign of acceptance, not farewell, have a good life separate from this man we all adore who's way out of your league. Right?"

She folded her freshly laundered clothing and stacked the folded items in her handbag.

From his seat at the foot of the neatly made bed in the previously wrecked guestroom, Marcus smiled. "Those were thank you Jesus hugs and kisses for easing their fears that I'll die alone as some weirdo reclusive sports footnote. They try to use Maddy and my nephews to lure me away from here, but I always use Mrs. Osgood, the media room, and the enclosed rooftop pool to convince the kids to visit me here instead."

"Well, if you're game for another outing, Marcus, dinner with my parents tomorrow night is at the old Black Door supper club in the Financial District at eight. Suit and heels dress code. Are you sure about this?"

Albany sat next to him so closely that they touched from shoulder to thigh to knee. With her left hand, she covered his right hand pressed flat against his thigh and wove her fingers between his while she waited for him to speak.

☙❧

Marcus wasn't sure of anything beyond his terrifying desire to spend more time with Albany even if he had to venture out into a completely unfamiliar public space to do so, even if the thought of going somewhere without knowing the dimensions or layout or furniture arrangement made him feel nauseated. He was going to fling himself back into a full life because he was tired of hiding, and exploring the possibilities with Albany was worth the risks.

"Yes, I'm sure."

Marcus suspected that Margeaux would gloat for the rest of her life.

CHAPTER 26

Because Jon had fallen asleep stretched out full-length on the sofa with his head in her lap, Margeaux suppressed her urge to shout for joy as she scrolled through gossip blogs and clicked links to breaking sports news about the unexpected return of Marcus Brandon Thomas to golf with critically acclaimed photographer A.M. Cole at his side during the inaugural fundraiser for Big Joe Huntsman's new philanthropic venture.

Most of the quotes from the other participants gushed about the surprise of Marcus's presence, the thrill of golfing with him, and being tutored by such a great golf talent. One person speculated that Marc wasn't really blind or that the man who had led his group to second place had been an imposter or a decoy.

Employees at the facility offered no comments while Big Joe Huntsman only thanked Marc for classing up the Huntsman Camps 4 Kids fundraiser with his presence.

No photos of Marc or Albany at the night golf event, but plenty of eyewitness descriptions. The consensus from the participants seemed to be that Marc's golf form was still a thing of enviable beauty, his patience infinite, and his scars reminded them of his courage in saving a pregnant teenager's life. They thought his girlfriend had acted supportive without smothering him.

A few sites tried to revive the false speculation from years ago that the pregnant teen had been Marc's jailbait girlfriend, but then and now his supporters obliterated the attempted smear campaign with the facts confirmed by the investigations conducted by the police, fire department, ATF, and Child Protective Services.

Steffie's protective older brother always refuted any salacious allegations with a succinct, "No. Not true" every time he was asked.

Margeaux glanced away from her tablet to her phone when it vibrated with an incoming text from Theresa Johnson-Cole.

>Albany's father and I have just made a donation to the LuxeLinks Club mentoring programs as thanks for your assistance.

>Thank you, Margeaux replied before turning off her

phone and her tablet, relaxing into the sofa, and closing her eyes.

Jon would wake her when he was ready to go up-stairs. They were finally re-establishing their domestic routine now that the week-long grand opening festivities were finished at the private LuxeLinks Beach Club in Oyster Glen Cove, Maryland. Her stellar team was smoothly handling daily operations with the understanding that Margeaux had direct access to every encrypted scheduling and reporting system. She and her sisters were also taking turns with making unannounced visits at least once each week.

The release of that vitriolic unauthorized biography had brightened the spotlight on the new beach club and reignited vigorous sales of Margeaux's older books, which had increased demand for her as a motivational speaker with a higher fee than she'd been paid for her last booking almost a year ago.

Chloe and Franklin were already banking royalties from their exclusive licensing agreement with the US Department of Defense for their high-tech ink and light bulbs.

So far, every attack launched by unidentified ene-mies against her family, their reputation, and their busi-ness had ultimately benefitted Margeaux and everyone she loved. Jon and his love and his family and friends added more of life's gifts because of these unknown ad-versaries.

Before she drifted to sleep, Margeaux hoped that the mean-spirited biography was their last attempt to destroy her. Constant vigilance was exhausting.

こうこう

"Let's just move on," the younger man said to his older mentor, who was running at maximum speed on the fully inclined treadmill in the gym on his oceanfront estate, which had been built by the older man's ancestors five generations earlier.

"We missed out on the land and on whatever intellectual property got them a lucrative contract with the government. When asked for comment about *The Feminist Madam Matchmaker of the Rich and Powerful*, she says, 'Satirical fiction doesn't interest me.' She says it every time.

"The Hirsch family's DNA must be slathered with a non-stick coating because allegations against them just make them sexier and more interesting to the public, and more marketable to advertisers.

"I told you that manufactured biography was a waste of time and money. Plus, we paid the hack ghostwriter who claimed to be a former LuxeLinks companion entirely too much money to self-publish the book as LL Escort Number Sixty-Nine."

The older man's feet kept pounding the treadmill with a stomping staccato.

"Well, can we cross LuxeLinks and the Hirsch family off of our list?" the younger man asked.

He watched the older man gradually slow his pace to a moderate walk, then lower the incline to horizontal before his mentor said, "One more attempt. If it fails, too, we'll move on to the next target."

CHAPTER 27
EPILOGUE

Albany sat next to Marcus in the back seat of his luxurious sedan while Osgood navigated the streets toward New York City's Financial District. Her new bangles chimed to the rhythm of the movement of her nervous hands until Marcus covered them under one of his hands spread across her lap.

"It requires nerves of steel to survive an invasion of Thomases, and you handled that beautifully yesterday, Albany. Why are you so nervous about facing your parents, the two people in your life who love you most?"

His calmly delivered question drew her thoughts away from her spiraling anxiety. While her feelings settled, Albany's gaze drifted over the compelling image

Marcus presented in the reflected glow of the city lights at dusk.

His locks were neatly braided into two long, inverted cornrows with the ends tucked into a plain black metal clip at the nape of his neck. The fashionable horn-rimmed glasses on his face weren't prescription or sunglasses, but the lenses were tinted gray to protect his eyes from strain. The frosty gray linen and silk fabric of his bespoke jacket accentuated the strong line of his straight shoulders as much as the stiff collar of his blue-black linen shirt framed his hard jaw.

She'd had the repeat pleasure of watching him shave earlier during her debate about which of the two new garments hanging on the closet door, two pairs of designer shoes, and complementary accessories to wear from the collection of purchases Mrs. Osgood had made for her from the nearest boutique.

Her plan to return to her side of her duplex in Lewisboro yesterday evening to prepare for her parents' inquisition changed when Albany was saying her good-byes to Marcus and his staff. Albany's next door neighbor had texted her that a few reporters were camped out in front of their converted farm house. That led Marcus to invite her to spend another night with him after she explained the reason for her sigh.

Now, sitting next to Marcus in the back seat of his car, Albany's sapphire blue, perforated lace tank dress with a flared skirt coordinated with the nude ankle-strap sandals and snake print fabric clutch without being too matchy-matching.

Mrs. Osgood's taste in fashion as armor was impeccable.

Albany finally felt calm enough to answer Marcus's question with complete honesty.

"My parents have poured all of their love and high expectations into me. I don't want their focused intensity to scare you away, Marcus."

He nodded slowly, then after traveling another block in silence he said, "You're the only person with the power to send me away at any time, Albany, by telling me that you don't want me. Otherwise, we're a team. Are we clear on that?"

"Crystal," she said as the car stopped under the portico for the Black Door Club.

CHAPTER 28

This Mark Flips the Script
The LuxeLinks Club Story 4

Twenty Years Ago:

John Snelling Hirsch sat at the antique marquetry table he'd inherited from his great-grandmother on his father's side of the family. Tonight it was covered with a game board loaded with plastic houses, hotels, and metal game pieces. Pastel-colored play money lay scattered about and stacked in messy piles. The game room was quiet because two-year-old Chloe had fallen asleep in his lap. Six-year-old Julianna was silently studying the board while she was leaning shoulder to shoulder with solemn eight-year-old Margeaux, who was studying the board with the concentration of a general preparing to conquer a hostile territory.

A lethargic and uncomfortable Franca had retired to bed immediately after dinner. Their son's due date was two weeks away.

When his oldest daughter finally decided to use all of her money to buy another hotel, John said, "Margeaux, whenever you risk everything you have, you need to be willing to lose it all and consider how much it will cost you to start again from nothing."

His oldest daughter looked up from the game board. Her huge eyes slowly blinked at him.

John breathed deeply, forcing himself to look into dark brown eyes that reminded him of his first wife, the mother of all three of his darling girls. The woman who had killed herself in despair in the aftermath of his multiple betrayals of her and their sacred vows seemed to be gazing at him through their oldest child's eyes.

"This is only a silly game, Daddy," she said very calmly, as if he were more than a little slow. "People are more important than games and things and money. Mommy taught me that."

CHAPTER 29

Present Day:

On day twenty-three of scouting his target, the freelancer watched the founders of HelioSun Tech Hub from the periphery of his vision as the man and the woman watched the boats, the birds, and the tourists enjoying the perfect summer day at the Inner Harbor in Baltimore City, Maryland.

Every weekday afternoon sometime between one and two-thirty, the tall welterweight man escorted his short, stacked business partner to lunch at one of the waterfront restaurants. In good weather, they sat on one of the benches near the edge of the docks. In bad, they patronized one of the second-story restaurants and hunkered down on one of the balconies enclosed in glass.

Their pattern supported the credible rumors that Kerry Anne Priest was now claustrophobic in addition to being publicly reserved.

The freelancer felt confident in his plan to kidnap the woman his client planned to use as leverage to control his target's business partner, William Jones.

Every evening between four-thirty and six, Jones tucked Kerry Priest into the backseat of a chauffeur-driven SUV with darkly tinted windows from a local hired car service to take her to her home on the other side of town from their Pratt Street offices before Jones returned to work or walked several blocks to his West Harbor condo.

The man usually changed into casual clothes before heading out for an evening of drinks and darts or pool with his rowdy guy friends at a nearby sports bar. Sometimes he spent his evenings at a dojo in the Woodberry neighborhood. The woman was always locked up in her small house for the night by seven.

On Saturday afternoons, Jones drove over to his partner's house to take her errand running and grocery shopping. They always returned before sunset then remained inside until they left for church the next morning. After brunch at a diner within walking distance of the church, Jones dropped off Priest by escorting her to her front door and kissing her until she needed to lean against the doorframe for support before he departed for his condo to start the new work week.

Their routine hadn't varied in the three weeks-plus of his surveillance.

The freelancer stood, letting his body ease into the flow of unsuspecting humanity and leaving the objects of his observations behind him for the rest of the day because tomorrow, Friday night, he would be waiting for Kerry Anne Priest inside her home.

ɛɔɛɔ

"Invite me to stay at your place tonight, Will," Kerry whispered into his ear once she'd leaned close enough to stamp his skin with her warm breath.

Will managed to swallow the last bite of his lunch without choking on the food or his surprise. "So you can smile sweetly at me while you say, No, thank you, Will. I'll see you on Saturday? Well, no, thank you, Kerry. Just tell me what you want from me, and I'll decide if I'm willing to give it to you."

ɛɔɛɔ

Kerry looked into the furious dark eyes of the brilliant, beautiful man she had loved since their freshman year in college. At first, she had greatly resented her randomly assigned roommate for essentially moving her boyfriend into their tiny ten square feet of space in the co-ed dorm, where it was impossible for Kerry to escape their continuous displays of affection or sounds of inter-course—while Kerry was in the room. Trying to sleep. Trying to study for the challenging general engineering weed-out courses in science and math.

After one interminable week of feeling condemned to showering and changing her clothes based on her roommate's and the boyfriend's absence, and being exiled to camping out in the communal dorm lounge or the library whenever Kerry wasn't in class, Kerry found out that Will was the boyfriend's roommate in the same dorm one floor higher.

The afternoon that she knocked on his door and realized that they were in two classes together started an association of convenience, which quickly evolved into a close friendship. Their romance took longer, but once established it survived Will's two years in Japan in an engineering training exchange program. Their relationship also survived their attendance at graduate schools on opposite sides of the country, including mutually agreed upon breaks.

And somehow, Will's love for her had deepened and strengthened in the aftermath of the incident two years ago that had triggered nearly debilitating claustrophobia and borderline agoraphobia in her, shrinking the boundaries of her world to suffocating dimensions.

Shared patents and business entanglements would keep them professionally linked to each other for years regardless of what happened with their romance, but Will had stayed by her side through all of it because he loved her. He had given her his whole heart years ago. It was past time for Kerry to demonstrate that the same truth was an immutable fact for her, too.

"I want the man I love to invite me to come over to his condo tonight so we can make love until we pass out from exhaustion. I want us to call in sick tomorrow to get an early start on spending our first weekend in bed since before my parents were killed in the mudslide that spared me from death while it condemned you to a life in limbo, waiting for me to recover fully."

She nuzzled her face against his neck and breathed him into the bottom of her lungs.

"I want to live a full life with you, Will. Am I too late?" she whispered.

ొ

Will felt Kerry's eyelashes brush his jaw. While steamy heat baked his skin faster than the weak breeze off the briny water could cool him, Will felt the soft press of her lips and her nose, and her breath tickle his neck, but he wasn't amused. He was unbalanced. Spinning between cautious optimism and unfulfilled expectations made him close his eyes against the glare of the sun and breathe.

ొ

Kerry waited. It was the least consideration she could offer to Will after all of the waiting he had done for her: to complete her doctorate; to get out of surgery, awake from a medically induced coma then rehab after surviving the mudslide; to grieve the loss of her parents; and then finally to overcome her phobias.

Waiting for Will to answer her question about their future was torture, but she sat silently next to him until he gently nudged her into sitting upright before he gathered up their lunch debris.

She watched him stand, then dodge between straggling tourists to reach the trash bin. On his return, Will sat turned toward her, but far enough away from her on the bench to leave space for another adult to sit between them.

Kerry held his gaze while he brought out his phone, then speed dialed without looking down.

"Hi, Ellen, this is Will," he said when the call connected. "Kerry and I aren't returning to the office today, and we're taking off tomorrow, too. Please tell the team that they're welcome to work from home tomorrow." He slid closer to Kerry until their knees bumped while he listened to their office manager. "Yes, set tomorrow's phone message and email auto-reply to 'Apologies for this unscheduled closure.' We'll resume our regular business hours on Monday…Yes…Our clients know to call me directly if they have a time-sensitive concern… Yes…You're welcome, Ellen…Thank you. We will."

He kept his eyes on Kerry, and his phone in his hand after the call ended. "Saturday nights and occasional quickies in our private office washroom have only whetted my hunger for you, Kerry. I'm ravenous for you. If you come home with me right now, that's it. We're forever. Engagement. Marriage. Kids."

His voice was calm. His gaze was turbulent.

Kerry reached out and placed her palm flat upon the jute linen fabric covering his tense muscular thigh. "You'd better plan a proper marriage proposal, William Jones, or else I'll just keep using your big brain for business, your big heart for emotional safety, and your big—" She let her gaze flick down to his lap, then back up to his eyes. "—endowment for my pleasure."

"Let's go indulge ourselves," he said.

CHAPTER 30

Sitting in the front seats on the Charm City Circulator shuttle next to the woman he had loved for all of his adulthood, Will found it hard to believe that his patience was being rewarded so suddenly after two long years of waiting.

Will's commitment to moderating a discussion panel at an annual STEM education symposium was the only reason he hadn't been injured like Kerry or buried alive like her parents in the catastrophic mudslide at the rustic-luxe rental cabin in the woods of Washington State. Every event since the frantic call from his parents about Kerry's medical flight to the nearest shock trauma unit after being dug out of an air pocket was embedded in his memory and still occasionally generated nightmares.

During the weeks of Kerry's surgeries and medically

induced coma, Will had used his reciprocal power of attorney with her for emergency healthcare situations to assert his authority to identify the bodies of Charles and Mary Anne Priest, and arrange for the embalming and storage of their remains.

He'd hired trustworthy house sitters for both Kerry's and her parents' Baltimore homes while trusting their small corporate team to run HelioSun Tech Hub as Will camped out at Kerry's hospital bedside or the cafeteria and prayed for a miracle.

Every morning and every night, Will thanked God and science for Kerry's life even though she was different in ways that were noticeable beyond the claustrophobia and agoraphobia.

Her IQ remained as high as ever, but her bubbly cheerfulness was less consistent and now offset by an underlying pensiveness, which she consciously worked to shake off.

Until today, Kerry had used her phobias and personality changes as reasons not to spend time with him outside of work after quitting time on weekdays.

After her final physical rehabilitation checkup six months ago, she had told him, "You've remained the same calm, loving, honorable, reliable man I've loved for years, Will, but I've changed. Take some time to decide whether or not staying with me as I am now is motivated by more than guilt, obligation, and habit."

Will had agreed, despite his fury, because he'd recognized the manifestation of Kerry's fears and new insecurities.

Today, Will glanced to his left and down into Kerry's twinkling eyes and answered her bright smile with his own as he gently squeezed her hand where it lay atop his thigh pressed to hers. He rejoiced in the evidence that simply remaining constant and not pushing her had resulted in the desired outcome.

✧✧✧

Seeing the uninhibited burst of joy in Will's smile that engaged his eyes and every muscle in his beloved face made Kerry recognize the fact that Will hadn't smiled so openly since the day she opened her eyes when her medical team brought her out of her restorative coma. Realizing that she hadn't noticed how much Will had been suffering made her feel selfish and deeply ashamed.

Eyes on his, Kerry tilted her chin up to angle her lips closer to Will's ear. He leaned sideways to close the gap between them.

Kerry whispered, "Let me take care of you this weekend, and for the rest of our lives, Will."

She interpreted the flare of sexual intensity in his eyes before he claimed her mouth in a voracious kiss as a yes.

✧✧✧

They stopped kissing long enough to get off at their stop two blocks away from Will's condo building. Their linked hands swung together in a short arc in the narrow space between them as they strolled toward their destination.

They returned the uniformed doorman's cheerful greeting when he opened one side of the heavy steel and glass double doors for them. Kerry and Will restrained themselves from additional public displays of affection through their smiling acknowledgement of the three receptionists and the wait for the elevator that would take them to Will's spacious unit, one of two on the top floor.

When the elevator doors closed, sealing them into the temporary false privacy of the rapidly ascending car, Kerry turned and stepped into Will's body. She wrapped her free arm around his waist. She sighed at the welcome weight of his free hand cupping the back of her head.

"If there weren't a security camera mounted in this elevator, Will, I'd straddle your thigh to ease this growing ache of emptiness between my legs. The same ache I feel every weeknight when I leave you at work and every Sunday when you leave me."

The hard nudge of his erection grew and prodded her below her rib cage.

"As soon as we're inside the condo, Kerry, feeling empty won't be a problem for you."

Will herded her out of the elevator before the doors glided fully open onto the wide hall.

☙❧

With his strong back to Kerry after he finished engaging the deadbolt lock, Will said, "If you like your underwear, Kerry, you have until I count down to one to remove them. Five. Four. Three." He turned, leaning against the solid door at his back while flexing his hands at his side like an Old West gunslinger. "Two. One."

Kerry remained still.

"This weekend is gentleman's choice, Will. It sounds like you want to rip off my clothes." She took the two steps that brought the front of her body flush against his. "Go for—"

Hard, strong hands grabbed her butt under the soft folds of her flared skirt and lifted her until her bare legs tightened around his waist while his firm lips pressed her mouth in an invitation to yield.

Will's open mouth devoured her. He tasted sweet and spicy from their shared lunch. He tasted hot and demanding as he hitched her clinging body lower against his crotch to align her vagina with his erection for a perfect jolt of pleasure when he crushed her between the wall at her back and his strong body plastered from her lips to her sopping wet vulva.

They both gasped when the need for air broke their kiss.

"Kerry," he said. "Look at me."

When she forced her heavy eyelids up, she met and

matched his fierce gaze without blinking.

"My gentleman's choice is you, marriage, and children. Immediately. We've accomplished everything we said we wanted to before settling down. No more condoms. Agreed?" The guttural depth of his voice matched the intensity of his gaze.

She hadn't been on birth control since the mudslide. And with his usual generous consideration for her welfare, he hadn't complained about using condoms again once she'd received the green light to resume sexual activities.

"No more condoms," she said.

The wattage of his sudden smile was as bright as the afternoon sun pouring into the condo from the wall of windows with an unobstructed view of the Inner Harbor marina.

❧❧❧

Will carried his future wife away from the wall next to his front door and deeper into the open living space, where he knelt on the antique silk and wool area rug Kerry had given to him as a housewarming gift for this spot in front of the gas fireplace. He lowered Kerry onto her back and followed her down, settling between her legs, but propping his upper body away from her chest by sliding his hands flat against the rug under her shoulders in a modified pushup, which allowed him to look down into her languid eyes.

"I need you hard and fast now to take off the desperate edge to fuck you senseless until you're pregnant." Without losing their direct eye contact, he slid back, sat up, and started stripping out of his cotton dress shirt as he knelt between her legs. He tossed the shirt over his shoulder before he unbuckled his belt and unfastened his pants. Once he'd shoved his linen pants and cotton briefs low enough to free his dick, Will reached down to pull Kerry's miniscule underwear down to the top of her splayed thighs.

"Your pussy is gorgeous."

ം

Kerry believed him.

Lying on the rug with her skirt hem bunched around her waist and her panties at mid-thigh, she recognized the greedy look in Will's eyes as his gaze repeatedly traced a visual loop between her eyes, her heaving breasts under the silky panels of her sleeveless wrap blouse, and the plump mound of her neatly trimmed mons.

The tip of his erection glistened as it bobbed above the tangle of fabric gathered at his hips. His gaze locked on hers again.

"Let's test your wetness, Kerry. Let's see if you're ready," he said, leaning and reaching forward with two fingers extended.

Will lifted off of his knees one at a time to rearrange

his bent legs to frame her straight legs. With the rough pads of his fingertips, he stroked the damp folds of her unfurled labia from bottom to top then taunted her clitoris with barely there brush strokes from side to side. The weight of his butt above her ankles immobilized her lower body, holding her in place while he played with her.

By the time he said, "Almost," then abruptly penetrated her with two fingers and tweezed them as he thrust them back and forth in her tight sex, Kerry's eyes were closed. Her back arched while her fingers clutched her head and tangled in her thick, loose hair. Her bare butt rubbed against silk and wool during her struggle to find the leverage to thrust her hips up high enough to help her move closer to orgasm.

"You said hard and fast, Will!"

His amused chuckle really annoyed her, but her irritation was forgotten when pressure from the blunt tip of his erection replaced his fingers, steadily pushing until she was stuffed full.

"Kerry."

His warm hands framed her face.

"Look at me, Kerry."

When their gazes locked, Will pumped his butt, claiming her as she lay there restrained by his legs braced alongside hers and by the scrap of fabric around her thighs. She untangled her fingers from her hair and reached up to frame his face between her cupped palms while he changed the angle of his thrusts to drag the length of his hard penis against her clitoris. That launched her primed body into orgasm a few frantic heartbeats before Will shoved deep and filled her with the hot rush of his orgasm. He shuddered and collapsed on top of her.

❧

Being able to breathe freely roused Kerry enough to realize that Will was stripping her panties down her legs and off the ends of her feet, still shod in her wedge-heeled sandals. She opened her eyes in time to watch the scrap of fabric float through the air to land on the heap of Will's discarded clothes since he was now completely naked.

"Yum," she said when all of his glorious anatomy hovered over her while he unfastened her skirt, untied her wrap blouse, but left her sheer lavender bra undisturbed.

Her clothes were haphazardly added to the pile on the floor behind Will. The nominal coverage of her sheer bra and peep-toed slingback sandals with cork wedge heels left her completely exposed. Will's eyes catalogued her face and her body as if he'd never seen her before this moment—as if they hadn't been lovers for more than a decade.

"I like seeing you overflowing with my sperm and knowing we're deliberately working toward conceiving a child."

He stretched out on top of her, using Kerry as a cushion. Staring down into her eyes, he framed her face in his hands.

"Open your legs. Give me your pussy again," he said, already pushing into her tender sex drenched in his ejaculate.

Her thighs cinched his waist and her ankles settled against the back of each of his thighs, leaving her pinned.

"Yeah, squeeze me with your hot, tight puss." His voice was little more than a guttural growl before his tongue filled her mouth the way his penis filled her vagina, both organs plunging deep until all she could do was hold on and let him take her into orgasm again, and again.

⁓⁓⁓

"Mercy," Will gasped as Kerry lapped her tongue around the head of his dick again—delicious payback for hours of his driving her from one peak to another in an inspired variety of ways.

Using his mouth, his fingers, and a feather on her had granted his body time to recover, but Kerry had cried lady's choice to give her swollen tissues and raw nipples a temporary reprieve.

Now he was the one who needed a break from having his body expertly driven into orgasm after being repeatedly teased close to the edge first.

"Seriously, Kerry, truce," Will said, grabbing her shoulders and pulling her up to lie against his sweaty side.

"Back to gentleman's choice: a nap, then dinner."

After a jaw-cracking yawn, Kerry said, "Deal."

കൗകൗ

Just before ten p.m., they got up to shower together and change the bed sheets. Each dressed in one of the complimentary robes from Will's collection acquired during years of hotel stays for STEM conferences.

Kerry and Will made a quick meal of roasted Gardein, tomatoes, and mushrooms on a bed of zucchini noodles. Afterward, he washed and she dried the few utensils, bowls, and plates.

Will cornered her against the door to the chef's pantry. His gaze held hers as he untied the fabric sash knotted at her waist. "Time for dessert," he said, pushing the overlapping robe lapels wide enough to frame her breasts, belly, mons, and legs without letting the supple material fall off of her shoulders.

His hands bracketed her waist, then slid down and back to squeeze her butt, lifting her onto the tips of her toes as his mouth descended to her breasts. He licked and suckled one nipple, then the other, back and forth as her fingers spread through his cap of tight, wooly curls. But she couldn't control him. She couldn't control his pacing or the strength of the suction he used to draw her nipples and the soft mass of her breasts deeply into the hot, damp catch of his hungry mouth.

Her sole focus on his mouth on her breasts fractured when the insistent press of his muscular thigh parted her legs and rubbed wash-worn silky cotton against her clitoris and vulva until she was straddling his thigh. Her toes no longer touched the floor as she rocked her crotch on his leg.

Although she felt too tender for more vaginal penetration, that didn't stop her clitoris from responding to the slick friction or her internal muscles from clenching in anticipation of being stretched. It didn't stop her from writhing on his thigh between her spread legs.

His fingers squeezing her butt clawed deeper and pulled, exposing her clenched anal aperture to the cool air.

"One finger or two, Kerry?" Will asked when he raised his head.

She blinked her eyes open, dazed, and frustrated, and desperate to come.

"One," she said, not surprised when one of his hands released her butt to lift his middle finger and press it into her mouth.

"Suck it just like you sucked my dick earlier today."

She did. Eyes on his, Kerry suckled his middle finger until it was wet from tip to base when he slid it out of her mouth.

"You're creaming more just from the thought of how I'm going to screw my finger into your tight asshole and finger fuck you into orgasm," he whispered as he lowered his hand and worked it under the back of the open robe.

She tensed at the soft tap of his wet fingertip, then breathed out hard when he pushed with more force to breach her and kept pushing until the entire length of his middle finger filled her rectum.

Anal play always revved her senses. This time was no different. In fact, Will's intensity heightened her pleasure in being pleasured by him in taboo ways.

His hand still squeezing her butt loosened its hold to allow him to cinch his arm tightly around her waist, sealing their upper bodies together from chest and breasts to hips.

With her hands still clutching his head, she had to tilt her chin up to maintain eye contact. His gaze drifted down to the quick rise and fall of her naked breasts for several heartbeats before returning to her eyes.

"Gentleman's choice, Kerry: first, my finger, then my dick."

Kerry's breath stalled in her chest. Since the dimensions of Will's anatomy made the mutual pleasures of anal intercourse very uncomfortable for her she usually only agreed to it on his birthday or to celebrate his major career achievements. She always came more than once in exchange for needing some time and a strategically placed ice pack to recover.

Kerry clenched her muscles as tightly as she could around the invasive finger and groaned at the jolt of provocative stimulation.

"Finger, lots of lube, then your erection, Will."

❦

He started plunging his finger back and forth in her super tight asshole, feeling primitive satisfaction as the wet spot on his thigh expanded while she rocked and moaned in his embrace, and pulled at his hair.

His dick felt harder than it had ever been in anticipation of taking the place of his embedded finger, which he shoved deeper.

Kerry stiffened with a high-pitched cry of Will's name and creamed all over his thigh before she collapsed into a trembling bundle of temptation in his arms.

Not wanting her asshole to close up, Will kept his finger inside her as he carried her back to the bedroom, where he lowered her feet to the floor near the top of the bed.

"Take off the robe, Kerry," he said as he shook free of one side of his robe until the garment dangled from the wrist on the same side as his finger plugged into her ass.

"Get the lube."

Kerry slowly leaned over to open the top drawer in the nightstand and picked out the package of cylindrical lubricant capsules designed for the rigors of anal penetration. They were as fat and long as a small adult's pinky finger. She removed the clear wrapper for one dose before she placed it in his free hand.

"Turn around and bend over with your elbows on the bed." After she complied, he gently tapped her inner ankles with his toes. "Spread them wider and bend your knees," he said, already easing the tip of the lubricant alongside the gradual withdrawal of his finger until the capsule slid inside and his finger slipped free.

He cupped her buttocks in the palms of his hands and squeezed them together before he said, "I'm going to wash my hands. Don't move."

❧❧

While Kerry felt the lubricant emulsifying inside her, she heard Will's retreating steps then running water before he came back.

She resisted the urge to look back over her shoulder at him as his continued silence gave her too much time to wonder about how he would sodomize her.

❧❧

Will loved looking at the delicate line of her shoulders and the sweet curve of her spine, which flowed into the two mounds of her irresistible ass. Her spread legs framed the juicy peach of her pussy. Her pose left her open and available for him to take in multiple ways.

Every time Kerry consented to being fucked in the ass, Will experimented with a different position and made mental notes about ease, comfort, and the ratio of pleasure to pain for her.

His inner Neanderthal preferred to take her with her knees on the bed with her head and shoulders flat against the mattress with one of his hands snared in her thick hair and the other hand pressed flat between her shoulder blades while he rammed her ass hard enough to make them both yell with each stroke.

Watching his dick slide in and out of her stretched asshole always got him harder and helped him last longer to maximize every nuance of pleasure in the rare sexual treat.

Vanilla sex with Kerry rated five out of five stars. Taboo sex with her was off the scale. Being in her presence, being invited into the sanctuary of her body always pleased all of his senses.

Tonight, he would choose a position that made him as vulnerable to her as she was to him.

⁓⁓⁓

"Kerry."

Will's hands gently grabbed her shoulders to pull her up and turn her toward him.

"Lie down on your back and lace your fingers on top of your head."

When she complied, Will stepped between her spread legs draped from her knees down over the side of the bed. He came down on top of her and hooked one of her knees over the crook of his arm, which tilted her hips to expose more of her butt. He nudged the blunt tip of his erection between her buttocks.

He propped his torso above her with his other arm.

"Look into my eyes, Kerry, and keep looking at me while I fuck you in the ass until you come."

He shoved, forcing her tight muscles to yield. Her breath stuttered at the sudden onset of the extreme discomfort of being stretched to accommodate his length and width in her rectum without any pause or chance of escaping the invasion of her body.

"Yeah, that's it," he said once he was fully sheathed in her anal chute. "Masturbate, Kerry."

His penis pulsed inside her, but he wasn't actively thrusting while she lowered her hands from the top of her head to stroke the plump, wet folds of her labia. Her protruding clitoris throbbed with engorgement, making her reticent to add more stimulation too soon.

"Add another," he said when she penetrated her tender vagina with one of her fingers.

She added a second finger and started pumping them into the wet heat of her narrow passage squeezed tighter by the fullness of being sodomized.

Switching his gaze from her eyes to her sex, Will otherwise held himself motionless while imminent orgasm surged through her body. When she started coming, he started lunging his hips, stretching and probing her depths with vigorous focus.

Kerry arched her back and shook her head from side

to side as she cried out in sexual distress. Pleasure and pain signals confused her senses while her body geared up toward another orgasm.

⌘

He wanted to capture her decadent sexual display in a photo, but Kerry had vetoed pictures and video of their sex life from the beginning of their relationship. He understood why, but would really appreciate preserving this image of her forever. Her eyes were closed, mouth open wide on an ecstatic scream, while her breasts jiggled and her supple belly undulated. One finger from each of her hands kept pumping her glistening bright pink pussy as he reamed her tight ass.

Will thrust balls-deep, then pushed deeper and unloaded into her snug chute with a full-throated roar.

⌘

After they recovered and cleaned up, Kerry and Will slept until early Friday afternoon.

⌘

Late Friday afternoon, the freelancer used the easement between the alley and the separate garages to approach the fenced backyard of Kerry's small, detached single-family cottage. He repositioned the two wide vertical slats he'd removed to access the tame garden space before he used his tools to break into her back door without leaving any outward evidence that he had done so. Bypassing the password demand at the prompt on the panel for her home security system was easy since he'd bribed a disgruntled IT worker at the company to tell him how to do it before the freelancer killed the traitor. He never trusted anyone who could be bribed.

Now all the freelancer needed to do was to wait for Kerry Anne Priest to come home.

He went upstairs and settled into a cozy reading chair in the corner of her bedroom with two rows of built-in shelves overflowing with a variety of hardcover, paperback, and leather-bound books.

 handing

"My back door just opened and closed, Will," Kerry said after she reached out and picked up her chirping phone from an accent table next to the sofa where she was sprawled sideways across his lap.

"Yes, I know, Kerry. Thank you very much."

She poked him hard in his side. "Not talking about that, perv."

They had fed themselves then dressed in weekend street clothes more than an hour earlier in preparation for heading out for a lazy afternoon as hometown tourists, but the urge to make-out had delayed their departure.

Will's gaze immediately sharpened as he sat up from his relaxed slouch. Kerry slid off his lap and sat up next to him.

"At your house?"

"Yes." She angled her phone so they could both watch the real-time moving images on the screen.

"What the hell?" Will whispered as they watched the intruder bypass the security code prompt.

Whatever the source of his information, it hadn't revealed the secondary code to deactivate her after-market modification.

"Well, at least we know that the prototype for our ten-eighty-degree surveillance thumbnail orb drone works in a real world scenario. And it must be completely silent because the intruder hasn't looked up or around at all."

"Yeah, there's that," Will said, then, "Do you recognize him, Kerry? I don't."

"No."

They watched the man dressed in dark jeans, golf shirt, and work boots explore the main level of her home before he glanced at the timepiece on his wrist and walked up the stairs to settle into Kerry's favorite chair after he shrugged off his backpack and placed it within easy reach on the floor near his feet.

In the span of a few seconds, Kerry heard Will string together more swear words—outside of sex—than he had spoken in her presence during all the years of their relationship.

"I think we should call the police, Kerry, but not nine-one-one."

She only nodded, unable to find her voice as they watched the intruder unzip his backpack and start methodically removing items: a gun with a silencer, a roll of duct tape, rope, a ball gag, a blindfold, scissors, and a black hood.

❧❦❧

Holy Mother of God, Will thought as he dialed the personal cell number for FBI Agent Howard Grimke, Senior, father of Howie, Will's best friend from their science and technology high school days. "Hi, Mr. Grimke, this is Will Jones…Yeah, yeah…Not so good, sir. My fiancée…Yes, Kerry. She and I have a situation…"

Will draped one arm across Kerry's tense shoulders and pulled her against his side as he talked to his best friend's dad while they watched the live feed of the intruder as the unknown man fastidiously repacked all of his gear except the gun.

"Yes, Mr. Grimke, you're sending Agent Marilyn Hoskins from the Baltimore City field office to meet us at my condo. ETA twenty minutes. I'll tell reception to expect her. Thank you so much…Yes, sir…Yes…Okay."

Will's arm tightened around her shoulders while they kept their eyes on the live video feed and waited.

ↄℐↄↄ

FBI Agent Marilyn Hoskins resembled Kerry in height, weight, complexion, and hair color, although the agent's hair length was much shorter.

After introducing herself and her four team members, they all crowded around Will's personal laptop, where Kerry had connected her phone to make the live video feed from her house easier for everyone to see.

The lead agent grilled them about their daily routine. She asked Kerry to sketch the layout of her home: main floor, second floor, and basement. Her team studied the view of Kerry's property on a satellite mapping app.

Agent Hoskins dialed her phone as she watched the intruder sitting with his gun in his lap while he read one of Kerry's books about low-tech solar power systems.

"Yeah, he's still inside. It's three-thirty now. The intended victim usually gets home between six-thirty and seven…Hold your position. Best play is for me to arrive as decoy at the residence in the expected hired car at six-forty, and enter the home, but I'll stay on the main level to see if I can draw him out…"

One of the other agents was furiously jotting notes onto a computer tablet as Agent Hoskins plotted strategy with whoever was on the other end of the connection.

By four o'clock, Agent Hoskins was dressed in a geometric print maxi dress and flat sandals from Kerry's emergency stash in Will's closet. A pale yellow scarf was tied around her head as a headband to hide her short hair. Kerry loaned her retro tortoise shell sunglasses and large silver hoop earrings to Agent Hoskins to hide her government agent stare and to give her a bohemian vibe.

"Okay, Will and Kerry, you two are staying here with Agent Lourdes Smith. The rest of my team and I are going to walk over to camp out at your office building until six when the car service you usually hire will pick me up—just in case the intruder has a spotter.

"Agent Muhammad Yankovic is most similar to you, Will, in body type and height so he'll escort me into the car as you would normally do for Kerry. Agents James and Rutherford will walk the area as tourists then follow us across town in vehicles that switch off from leading and trailing us to Kerry's house. Kerry, I won't answer any calls from anyone other than law enforcement while I have your phone. We're going to catch this suspect and find out who he is and what his intentions are. Let's roll."

Kerry and Will sat cuddled up next to each other on the sofa set perpendicular to the chair in which Agent Smith sat leaning forward with rounded shoulders to work from a frayed spiral notebook, a computer tablet, and a laptop arranged on the surface of the huge block of wood used as a coffee table in Will's living area. The agent wore headphones with one side skewed away from her ear so she could hear final instructions from Agent Hoskins before the decoy team left.

Kerry and Will held hands and waited.

⌖⌖⌖

The freelancer hated waiting. Another glance at his watch showed six-thirty-seven, two minutes later than the last time he'd checked. During three weeks of recon, his target had never arrived home later than seven, which meant only twenty-three more minutes max until he bagged the other half of his delivery fee.

Hearing the sound of a key in the lock on the front door made him smile.

⌖⌖⌖

As Marilyn Hoskins waved off the hired driver and entered the tidy little house, she reminded herself that, even without Kevlar and Graphene, she had the protection of the weapon in her clutch handbag with a fully charged Taser molded into the outside panel. The belt loosely looped at her hips was laced with a GPS tracker and listening device that allowed every member of her expanded tactical team to hear what she was hearing since Kerry's surveillance prototype wasn't configured to broadcast sound. The belt also functioned as a restraint with strong suction cups on each end camouflaged as decorative medallions. Marilyn had those tools, highly trained backup, and the element of surprise.

Her team could see what she was seeing on Kerry's phone because the intended victim had given them temporary access to the private site dedicated solely to recording the beta testing video for this particular prototype.

Marilyn's team would come for her at the first sign or sound of trouble.

On the small screen of Kerry's phone, Marilyn watched the suspect remain seated with his arms extended and his gun in the two-handed grip of a serious professional. She needed to draw him downstairs.

Marilyn kicked off her borrowed sandals before she headed toward the only bathroom in the house. Its location on the main floor suited the plan she had been considering and revising since her first look at Kerry's layout sketch. She entered the small space and closed the door tightly behind her before she started the shower.

◈◈◈

The freelancer waited until the shower had been running for a full minute after he heard the metallic drag of shower rings on the shower rod twice before he eased up from the very comfortable chair.

This little smarty-pants creampuff was making his job easy with her predictable schedule, solitary living arrangement, no pets, and unimpressive home security setup. Catching her in the shower would save him the time and effort of forcing her to strip. If only every target co-operated this much, he thought as he tiptoed down the short flight of stairs. A narrow hall linking two small rooms led to the tightly closed door of the bathroom.

The freelancer grasped the knob and slowly turned it until the hasp disengaged. He swung the door wide with one hand, taking a big step forward to sweep aside the dark denim shower curtain with his free hand.

Piercing pain in his back barely proceeded a shock-ing jolt to his entire body that made his limbs dance and jitter as he convulsively squeezed the trigger guard, dropped to his knees, and banged his head on the edge of the tub when a compact weight dropped onto his back, nearly broke his fingers while disarming his twitching digits, and Mirandized him while she zip-tied his wrists behind his back. She also managed to zip-tie his flailing ankles while what sounded like a stampeding herd of buf-falo swarmed into the house.

↩↩

"My boss thinks she's Spiderwoman," Agent Smith muttered loudly enough for Kerry and Will to hear the horrified awe in her voice. In a louder tone, the agent said, "Okay, Ms. Priest, your home is secure, and the suspect is in custody. Some of your neighbors have posted grainy video of the team entering your house then exiting with the suspect. Agent Hoskins is still posing as you to keep your location a secret. She'll come back here in a few hours as herself with Yank, James, and Rutherford." Smith paused. "You still with me, folks?"

Dazed, Kerry and Will simply nodded.

೧೧೧

"Is everyone under the age of forty a *moron*?" the older man screamed as he stomped back and forth in front of his certified reproduction of The Resolute Presidential Desk in his home office.

The younger man was listening, but he kept his eyes turned toward the desktop where a laptop was streaming a replay of breaking news from a local Baltimore City news site.

"He came highly recommended by people I respect. And he gets himself caught! How? We paid him a lot of money." The older man stopped pacing to stare down at the younger man. "Well! How are you going to fix this?"

The younger man did not say, I told you so. He didn't rehash the points of his earlier arguments against this poorly conceived idea to kidnap Kerry Anne Priest in order to force her business partner and lover, William Jones, to sabotage the solar energy system that their company, HelioSun Tech Hub, had installed and still maintained for the LuxeLinks Beach Club in Oyster Glen Cove, Maryland, simply for spite.

Being unable to discredit Margeaux Carr Hirsch, her LuxeLinks Club, and its members had completely unhinged the older man from sane thinking.

It was past time for the younger man to end his association with this nut. "There's nothing to fix. The prepaid phones we've used were bought with cash from different bodegas with broken security cameras. I never touched the prepaid phones with my bare hands, and now they're being used or being sold by the two different thieves who 'pickpocketed' me on the subway about an hour ago before I headed here when I first saw the news about the activity at Kerry Priest's house. We're safe. That captured man doesn't know our names. He's never seen our faces. Let's suspend further projects. Let things cool down."

Seeing the older man nod then calmly walk around his massive desk to sit in the matching replica chair reassured the younger man about his good odds of escaping to Panama to live the rest of his life very comfortably supported by the salary he'd mostly saved and the funds he'd skimmed off the top of every financial transaction he'd brokered on the older man's behalf.

The younger man was now quite wealthy. He had no intentions of missing out on retiring before his thirtieth birthday. Knowing that, by this time tomorrow, he would be sipping drinks on a powdery white sand beach in Panama, the younger man said, "We're safe even if the kidnapper betrays us. He knows nothing about us."

CHAPTER 31

He's not talking," Agent Hoskins said after they were all seated in Will's open living area at midnight. "He hasn't asked for a lawyer or water or food. He doesn't answer questions, but we know his name and his extensive criminal history because his prints were in the national database. The good news is that he always works alone. We also found more physical evidence of his criminal intentions toward you in the minivan he parked two streets north of your house."

Agent Hoskins paused and reached into her open messenger bag on the floor next to her chair. "And there's this," she said, extending one white sheet of copier paper toward Kerry and Will.

Kerry leaned closer to see the page when Will easily grabbed it with his longer arm.

The past nine hours had delivered a parade of shocking developments, and the words they were reading on the photocopied page continued the disturbing pattern. Each letter and number was torn from magazines and newspapers to spell out the ominous message: *Use this phone to call 011-52-555-9108 to save Kerry's life. No police or she dies a slow, hard death. Call no later than 1 p.m.*

Kerry and Will looked at each other, then over at Agent Hoskins, who said, "The original note was taped to a prepaid cell phone. Everything suggests that his plan was to overpower you inside your house then wait until dark to transport you to his minivan. We found a five-feet-by-two-by-two footlocker in the cargo area. He's clearly been watching you two enough to know that Will arrives at your house between twelve-thirty and one on Saturdays. The suspect must have…"

Kerry's brain could no longer focus on deciphering the words Agent Hoskins was saying because imagining how panicked she would have felt being tied up, blindfolded, gagged, and hooded before being stuffed into a dark footlocker that was too short for her to stretch out full-length had her gasping for breath as she remembered being immobilized and blinded by a surging wave of mud.

Unlike her parents who had been buried alive in the hot tub on the lower deck of the rental cabin, Kerry had been swept off the upper balcony and tumbled down the mountain slope along with a slurry of mud, trees, and building materials. She'd landed with a massive tree trunk at her back and some kind of metal structure crumpled around her with enough space between the two objects to create an air pocket.

Kerry remembered having an excruciating headache as she used a tree branch to bang on the metal. By the time search and rescue dug her free, she'd been encapsulated in a murky, pungent pod of darkness for more than three hours that felt like weeks to her scrambled brain inside her fractured skull.

Phantom memory of so much pressure behind her eyes blinded by the pain of her injury and the fetid muck of darkness that entombed her made her feel the start of nausea.

Gentle pressure guiding her head down between her knees brought her out of her flashback of her traumatic past experiences and forward into the present moment.

Will's calm voice said, "That's right, Kerry. Fill your lungs—one, one thousand, two, one thousand, three, one thousand, four—to slow your breathing, and hold your breath for four. Now exhale for a count of four then hold for four."

When Kerry sat up straight again, she appreciated the fact that Agent Hoskins and her team weren't looking at her like she was a mentally unstable freak.

Agent Yankovic offered Kerry a glass of water while Agent Hoskins said, "So my rush to tell you details before they leaked to the media outlets totally ignored what you told me about your claustrophobia and panic attacks since the mudslide. Forgive me?"

"Of course." Kerry nodded. "That's the first time that just hearing someone describe the possibility of my being confined in a small, dark space flipped me out. I hope it's a one-off."

Agent Hoskins nodded. "Feeling fear about someone's invasion of your home as part of their plan to kidnap you and hold you for ransom is a sane response."

The other three agents nodded then started packing up their tech gear while Agent Hoskins finished briefing Kerry and Will.

Agent Smith said, "We've saved the day's video feed from your surveillance drone prototype, but please give me a heads-up when you shut down our access to the site."

Kerry shared a look with Will before she said, "I won't shut down your access because we built it as an isolated site that's completely segregated with an instantaneous boomerang firewall collapse on the source of any hacking breach. I remotely deactivated the drone after the last member of the evidence team locked up. Do you need the actual drone for your investigation?"

Agent Hoskins said, "No," then she waved off Kerry and Will as they started to rise from the sofa in order to open the door for the departing team. "We'll see ourselves out. You two get some rest and don't worry. I'll keep Agent Grimke in the loop. Call Grim if you have questions. Otherwise, you're clear of this. Thank you for helping us take a very bad man out of circulation."

∽∾∽∾

In the abrupt silent stillness after a last round of more thanks, goodbyes, and best wishes before the condo door closed behind the last agent to leave, Will tightened his arm around Kerry's shoulders and squeezed her closer.

Remaining silent while Kerry conversed with Agent Hoskins had allowed the woman he loved to exercise a small measure of control during the conclusion of their part in this scary fiasco. It had also allowed his imagination too much time to generate a variety of possible outcomes if Kerry hadn't propositioned him yesterday at lunch. If he hadn't spontaneously decided that they needed to take off the rest of the week for a long weekend, what would the intruder have done when Kerry wasn't home as expected? All of the possibilities equaled something bad for Kerry.

"Will," she said. "Will, ease up on the anaconda hold. I'm not going anywhere."

He immediately relaxed his muscles as he looked down at her, cuddled up under his arm. "Why were you ready yesterday to accept that my love for you is eternal? I love the woman you are now even more than I loved the woman you were before the mudslide, coma, speech therapy, physical rehabilitation, and phobias. What made you finally believe me, Kerry?"

A rueful smile curved her plump lips. "Margeaux called to check up on me last Sunday night a few minutes after you left. She said it was to confirm my site visit to her LuxeLinks Beach Club in August and the tentative schedule for my interview and photo shoot with A.M. Cole for her Powerful Subjects series. Toward the end of the conversation, she asked me what I would have done if you had been the one critically injured in the mudslide. Would I have camped out at your hospital bedside for months, playing your favorite tunes softly in the background? Would I have delegated all business travel to other members of the team and run our company from the corner of your private hospital room, after calling in favors to get you transferred to The Baltimore University Medical Center?

"Margeaux asked me if I would have stopped loving you or loved you less. I told her no, all of that would have made me love you more—appreciate you more." Kerry shifted and pushed against Will, surprising him and toppling him onto his back on the sofa with Kerry lying breasts to chest on top of him. She cupped his face between the soft palms of her graceful hands. "The first time I saw you when I came out of the coma, Will, your beautiful smile didn't keep me from seeing how gaunt and exhausted you were." She brushed her lips across his, then pulled back to frown at him. "Because of me," she whispered. "What if I can never drive again, Will? Have you really considered how much of a hassle that's going to be for you, especially once we have kids?"

He inhaled a big breath then spoke the deepest truth of his heart. "Being spared from marking the anniversary of your death with memories and flowers at a gravesite is worth whatever is required of me, Kerry."

He'd never shared the specific warnings her doctors and nurses had given him multiple times about her slim odds of surviving and the high probability of permanent neurological and physical impairment. Her phobias, scars, and slight limp when she was very tired were negligible measured against his gratitude for her continued existence as the brainy, ambitious, funny, impatient woman he loved.

ᎾᏕᎾ

Kerry stared down into Will's face, keeping her eyes locked on his as she absorbed the power of his love for her.

His constant support had anchored her and bolstered her and cheered her. Often, it had prodded her to dig deeper into previously untapped reserves of faith, stamina, and endurance. Kerry thought she probably would have survived the mudslide without him, but not with as much joy and optimism.

"Thank you for not rushing me, Will."

"Six months in exchange for a lifetime commitment with you is the best return on investment of my life, Kerry. "Now kiss me to seal the deal."

She laughed. "Is that the secret to your one-hundred-percent contract closing rate with our clients, Will—kisses?"

He smiled as he gently cupped the back of her head with one hand to tug her lips closer to his mouth. "Travel with me to meet our next prospective client and find out," he said before their parted lips clashed in a soft collision of supple flesh, seeking tongues, and sharp teeth.

Kerry pulled back and smiled. "Okay, Will, time to line up everything you need for my marriage proposal. Are we ring shopping together, or are you going solo?"

"No," he said.

"No, what?"

"No ring shopping necessary. I bought your ring two years ago."

CHAPTER 32

As Kerry stared mutely down into his face, Will silently debated with himself about how much more truth to tell. "My parents and I were already scheduled to fly out to Washington State on the night of the mudslide. I'd arranged for other engineers to cover my panel discussions for the last two days of the conference. We were planning to spend the night at the nearest bed and breakfast then get to the rental cabin in time for breakfast with your family the next day. That's how we got there so quickly after the disaster."

Will felt the heat of a blush fill his face as he said, "In my mind, we were already committed for life. We just needed to make it legally binding. When I invited your dad to lunch about a month before your family's back-to-nature vacation, he said that no man would ever be good enough for his baby girl, but he thought I had all the makings of a worthy candidate. Your mom helped me narrow the ring choices down to three, then she said she was removing herself from the final decision because she wanted to be surprised along with everyone else during the proposal."

He surrounded Kerry's face between his palms. "So during these past six months when you've been giving me time and space to leave you, Kerry, I've felt like a husband who's being involuntarily separated from his wife."

"Oh, no, Will." He read the words from her lips more than he heard the actual words whispered in her teary voice.

∾∽∾∽

Seeing tears drop one slow, small splash at a time onto Will's face made Kerry realize that the pressure behind her eyes and in her full to bursting heart was making her cry with relief. And more than a little shame for not understanding how much she had unintentionally hurt Will for loving her through the best and the worst.

"I love you," she said between darting kisses to his nose and scruffy cheeks. "I love you so much, Will," she said before she locked her lips to his and devoured him.

She poured all of her love for him into his mouth with her parted lips and sweeping tongue, while lower between their bodies his hands unfastened his jeans and shoved them down before reaching under her straight knit skirt to wrestle her panties low enough on her legs for him to shove them free with his bare foot. His hands drifted up to her hips, pulling up the hem of her skirt until air-conditioned coolness hit her exposed butt.

She shivered as he raised her lower body to hover above his crotch. He turned his head, breaking their kiss.

"Guide me home, Kerry."

She slid her bare legs along the outside of his denim-clad thighs and knelt astride his strong body as his hands still bracketed her hips.

With her eyes holding his gaze, Kerry wrapped both of her hands around the hot, damp thickness of his erection and squeezed with enough pressure to make him groan. But he didn't close his eyes as he lifted her up and forward to center her vagina over the blunt, weepy tip of his penis.

Slowly, she lowered herself, pausing to savor the menacing nudge of his cockhead between the wet folds of her labia before she slid lower on a breathy sigh as her body stretched to receive him. She kept sinking lower until they were sealed together groin to mons.

When Kerry slowly leaned forward to rest her hands against his chest covered in the threadbare cotton of a science conference t-shirt, they both moaned at the sensations sparked by the shift in the angle of their connection.

"Yeah, fuck me like that," he growled when her internal muscles clamped down hard on the pulsing hot length of implacable flesh invading her and stretching her.

The flat of his hand slapped one side of her butt with enough force to startle her with its sting.

"Ride me, Kerry. Ride me hard and fast."

She did. Eventually.

First, she rocked her hips, treating him like her personal human hobby horse and tormenting them both with her slow pace and limited range of motion. She resisted the urging of his hands squeezing her butt to hurry her.

Their private office washroom quickies always provided fleeting satisfaction whether Kerry was bent over the vanity with her skirt held gathered at her waist as Will pumped furiously fast, or he was seated on the closed commode with Kerry astride. Sometimes he only teased her with his mouth when he was frustrated with her. Quick, furtive sex with him during the week had taken off some of the edge until their Saturday night sex fests, which she preferred because she liked taking her time with him to indulge all of their senses without needing to watch the clock or listen out for their staff.

She and Will were now going to have the rest of their lives to indulge themselves in the best of both worlds.

"Thank you," she whispered as she leaned down to kiss him.

CHAPTER 33
EPILOGUE

Three Years Later:

High-pitched childish shrieks and giggles filled the air on the long stretch of private beach as playground for the intimate group of children and their parents, who were wading through the soft wash of low tide, flying kites, building sand castles closer to the canopied sun deck, and chasing or being chased by other members of their select group.

Kerry sat next to Margeaux in the middle of a row of cushioned chaise loungers, each with its own oversized umbrella staked behind it.

Both women watched the melee of families they

loved having fun in the sunny humidity.

Kerry said, "Did you have Agent Tiptree hypnotized into temporary docility to get him to approve this trip for you, Margeaux? Last time we talked you said Jon vetoed the trip as too close to your due date."

Margeaux rolled her head to the left to frown at Kerry.

"True, but my doctor convinced him that a few hours' drive from New York to Maryland would not shake our first baby out of my womb at thirty weeks. Jon agreed as long as I agreed to do absolutely nothing more strenuous than slather myself in sunscreen.

"Oh, and modest walks along the shoreline before nine a.m. and after six p.m. are also permitted."

Kerry laughed as her eyes swept over the people on the beach.

"Well, I'm glad your husband's concerns didn't keep you from attending this reunion of happily married LuxeLinks couples. Thanks for letting us crash your party."

Margeaux waved off Kerry's words with a delicate slicing motion of her hand as she said, "You and Will are honorary members by virtue of all of the clean energy systems installations and maintenance HelioSun provides for our professionally incestuous network."

Kerry laughed. "Well, it is very nice to spend a week at the beach with good friends at a private waterfront club that's closed for a month for interior design renovations.

"What did your other members say when you noti-fied them that the beach club was going to close for a month—in August?"

"Nothing. They've all got getaway homes on The Vineyard or in The Hamptons, Aspen or on the west coast, in Hawaii and around the world. This little place is just a convenient location and comfortable spot for mel-low networking events and a good place to bring young people for our mentoring programs and retreats." Margeaux's voice trailed off. Very quietly, she said, "I think my mom would have approved."

Kerry reached over and squeezed her friend's hand. "She definitely would have, Aunt Ma-gogo."

Both women started laughing on the last syllable of Kerry's squeaky mimicry of two-year-old Charlotte Anne Priest-Jones's name for her godmother and honorary aunt.

Kerry continued holding Margeaux's hand as they watched Beck catch Alexa around her bare waist, lift her off her feet, then run into the surf despite her half-hearted struggles and laughing protests.

A chorus of "Me, too! Me, too!" started from the gaggle of small to lanky jumping children now gathered around Will, Jon, Jon's sister Elizabeth, and Marc while Albany used her designated limit of five minutes per hour to snap photos.

Albany's husband shamelessly indulged his wife's every request, except for her desire to hide behind her camera even when she wasn't working.

Will scooped up Charlie. Jon grabbed up his younger niece and nephew, then both men charged into the water near Alexa and Beck with a roar that had their helpless captives screaming and giggling, but not struggling very hard to escape. Albany just kept circling and working camera angles as she ignored her husband's dramatic pleas for rescue when Jon's older niece and nephew each claimed one of Marc's hands and dragged him into the water with the squealing, splashing group.

Margeaux tugged her hand free of Kerry's to make shooing motions toward the frolickers. "Go get in the water, Kerry. I'll be fine. Promise."

Kerry shook her head and looked at her pregnant friend like she was crazy. "No way, pregnant lady who fainted into her husband's arms and scared an inch off his considerable height. You know our marching orders from Agent Hard Ass: Margeaux is never left alone on the beach. The lifeguard doesn't count."

Kerry's annoyed pregnant friend huffed and glared out toward her husband's location in the water, then turned her head to glare at Kerry again.

"I fainted once during my first trimester because I was anemic, exhausted, dehydrated, and unaware that I was pregnant." Her last few words were shrill, even though she hissed them subvocally.

Kerry held up her hands in surrender. "I'm not the person you need to convince. That would be your bossy, overprotective husband, who has managed to become bossier and more overprotective during your pregnancy.”

"I know!” Margeaux flounced back against the plush lounge cushion. “He's supported his sister through all four of her pregnancies. First, while his brother-in-law drove tractor trailer hauls across the country, then when he was in and out of rehab for substance abuse. I expected Jon to be the laid-back parent and for me to be the obsessive one.”

Kerry heard the teariness in Margeaux's voice and saw the glossy sheen of wetness in her eyes. “No. No crying, Ma-gogo.” She surreptitiously slipped a new handkerchief into her friend's hand from the supply she'd ordered, same-day shipped to the beach club and started carrying on the first day of their reunion. “If your husband finds out that I made you cry, he'll erase me from existence with the incendiary force of his stare.”

Kerry demonstrated, which made Margeaux laugh on the tail end of a watery gurgle.

“Oh, thank God,” Kerry said as they both smiled and waved at Jon, who had turned and taken three steps toward them as if his niece and nephew were not respectively clinging to his waist and perched on his shoulders like human barnacles.

“He reads my moods like he's a mind reader, Kerry. It's freaking me out,” Margeaux whispered after sipping some water from a thermos filled with ice.

“You're his pregnant mate. This is your first child, and Jon would swim across the ocean without a shark cage, jump from a plane without a parachute, walk through fire, chew glass or go shopping at an outlet mall on the day after Thanksgiving to keep you safe and healthy. Just roll with it. Soon you'll both be too sleep-deprived to argue about anything."

Margeaux laughed. "Nice pep talk, wise mommy coach."

Kerry smiled. "Just the same cold, hard truth Will's mom shared with me when she invited herself to live with us for the first month of Charlie's life. I agreed for the sake of family diplomacy and harmony with my in-laws. The second night of being home from the hospital with Charlie, I closed myself in the bedroom closet and fell to my knees and thanked God for my mother-in-law's fore-sight.

"On top of being overwhelmed by Charlie and moth-erhood, grief for the loss of my parents—especially my mom, kept surging up in sudden waves at weird times.

"By the time Prudence left, I felt more emotionally settled. Will and I both felt relatively confident that Char-lie would survive in our care."

Margeaux nodded slowly. "Thank you for sharing that, Kerry. My mom has been prominent in my thoughts more than usual.

"We're totally moved into Jon's home in Scarsdale. Since he's planning to take his full twelve weeks of fami-ly leave once I start labor, I've put off accepting his mom's offer to come over for a few hours every day during the first week or so."

Kerry nodded. "Accept your mother-in-law's offer. Your reticence is understandable, but it's much easier to have her there as a safety net, while you let her see that you won't drop her new grandchild on the head, than to need her support and not have her there and also feel too embarrassed to tell her you've changed your mind.

"Line up your team now, Margeaux, because when your baby arrives you won't care about anything else."

Weepy again, Margeaux nodded. "I just want to be a good mom, Kerry."

"You're going to be, Margeaux. You're a loving daughter, a loving sister, a loving friend, a loving wife, and person. You're going to be a loving mother, too. You're strong, and so is Jon. You've already laid a strong foundation for creating a healthy family and a long, rewarding life.

"Your mother was a loving mom who would want more for you than what she accepted for herself.

"Okay?"

"Yes."

⌘

Two days following her parents' return to Scarsdale, New York from their vacation retreat in Oyster Glen Cove, Maryland, Sidney Carr Tiptree burst into the world on an unseasonably cold evening in late August, during the thirty-third week of her mother's pregnancy. Eleven hours of labor, two days in the hospital for Margeaux, and three weeks for the baby made Jon happier and bossier and more overprotective than ever. It also made him more loving than he'd imagined he could be.

About the Author

C. X Brooks is a hopeful romantic who believes in love that endures and deepens. She is a reading fiend, compulsive writer, chocoholic, travel geek, swim enthusiast, and fan of exercises that work well in bare feet. Her goal as an author is to expand the variety and volume of upbeat, diversity-is-mainstream contemporary erotic fiction about grown-ups in love.

She also writes as Cardyn Brooks. Find her on Amazon, Facebook, Goodreads, SheWrites, Smashwords, and Tumblr. Her book reviews are available at MediaDiversified.org.

www.ingramcontent.com/pod-product-compliance
Lightning Source LLC
Chambersburg PA
CBHW060951120726
47910CB00002B/589